Rascal
DOES NOT DREAM
of a
Dreaming
Girl
Hajime
Kamoshida
Illustration by
Keji Mizoguchi
T0047184

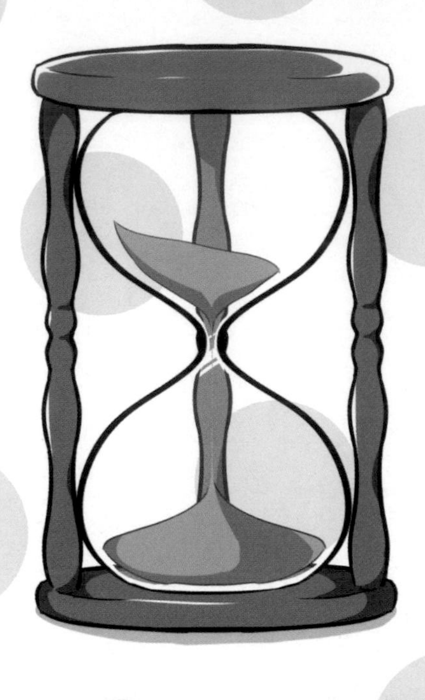

"Welcome home, Sakuta."
Shouko Makinohara
A mysterious older girl who was Sakuta's first love. When Sakuta needs help, she appears out of nowhere. Unbeknownst to Mai, she's currently living with Sakuta?!
When he gets home, she greets him like they're newlyweds. But what secrets is she hiding?!

“So don’t you go panting after any other women.”
Mai Sakurajima
A famous actress and Sakuta’s girlfriend. Third-year at Minegahara High. Her current goal is to meet Sakuta’s parents formally.
Will the appearance of Sakuta’s first love cause a rift in their relationship?

Rascal DOES NOT DREAM of a Dreaming Girl

Hajime Kamoshida

Illustration by
Keji Mizoguchi

New York

Rascal Does Not Dream of a Dreaming Girl
Hajime Kamoshida

Translation by Andrew Cunningham
Cover art by Keji Mizoguchi

SEISHUN BUTA YARO WA YUMEMIRU SHOJO NO YUME WO MINAI Vol. 6

Edited by Dengeki Bunko
First published in Japan in 2016 by KADOKAWA CORPORATION, Tokyo.
English translation rights arranged with KADOKAWA CORPORATION, Tokyo through TUTTLE-MORI AGENCY, INC., Tokyo.

Yen On
150 West 30th Street, 19th Floor
New York, NY 10001

Visit us at yenpress.com
facebook.com/yenpress
twitter.com/yenpress
yenpress.tumblr.com
instagram.com/yenpress

First Yen On Edition: November 2021

Library of Congress Cataloging-in-Publication Data
Names: Kamoshida, Hajime, 1978– author. | Mizoguchi, Keji, illustrator.
Title: Rascal does not dream of bunny girl senpai / Hajime Kamoshida ; illustration by Keji Mizoguchi.
Other titles: Seishun buta yarō. English
Description: New York, NY : Yen On, 2020. |
Contents: v. 1. Rascal does not dream of bunny girl senpai —
v. 2. Rascal does not dream of petite devil kohai —
v. 3. Rascal does not dream of logical witch —
v. 4. Rascal does not dream of siscon idol —
v. 5. Rascal does not dream of a sister home alone —
v. 6. Rascal does not dream of a dreaming girl
Identifiers: LCCN 2020004455 | ISBN 9781975399351 (v. 1 ; trade paperback) |
ISBN 9781975312541 (v. 2 ; trade paperback) | ISBN 9781975312565 (v. 3 ; trade paperback) |
ISBN 9781975312589 (v. 4 ; trade paperback) | ISBN 9781975312602 (v. 5 ; trade paperback) |
ISBN 9781975312626 (v. 6 ; trade paperback)
Subjects: CYAC: Fantasy.
Classification: LCC PZ7.1.K218 Ras 2020 | DDC [Fic]—dc23
LC record available at https://lccn.loc.gov/2020004455

ISBNs: 978-1-9753-1262-6 (paperback)
978-1-9753-1263-3 (ebook)

1 3 5 7 9 10 8 6 4 2

LSC-C

Printed in the United States of America

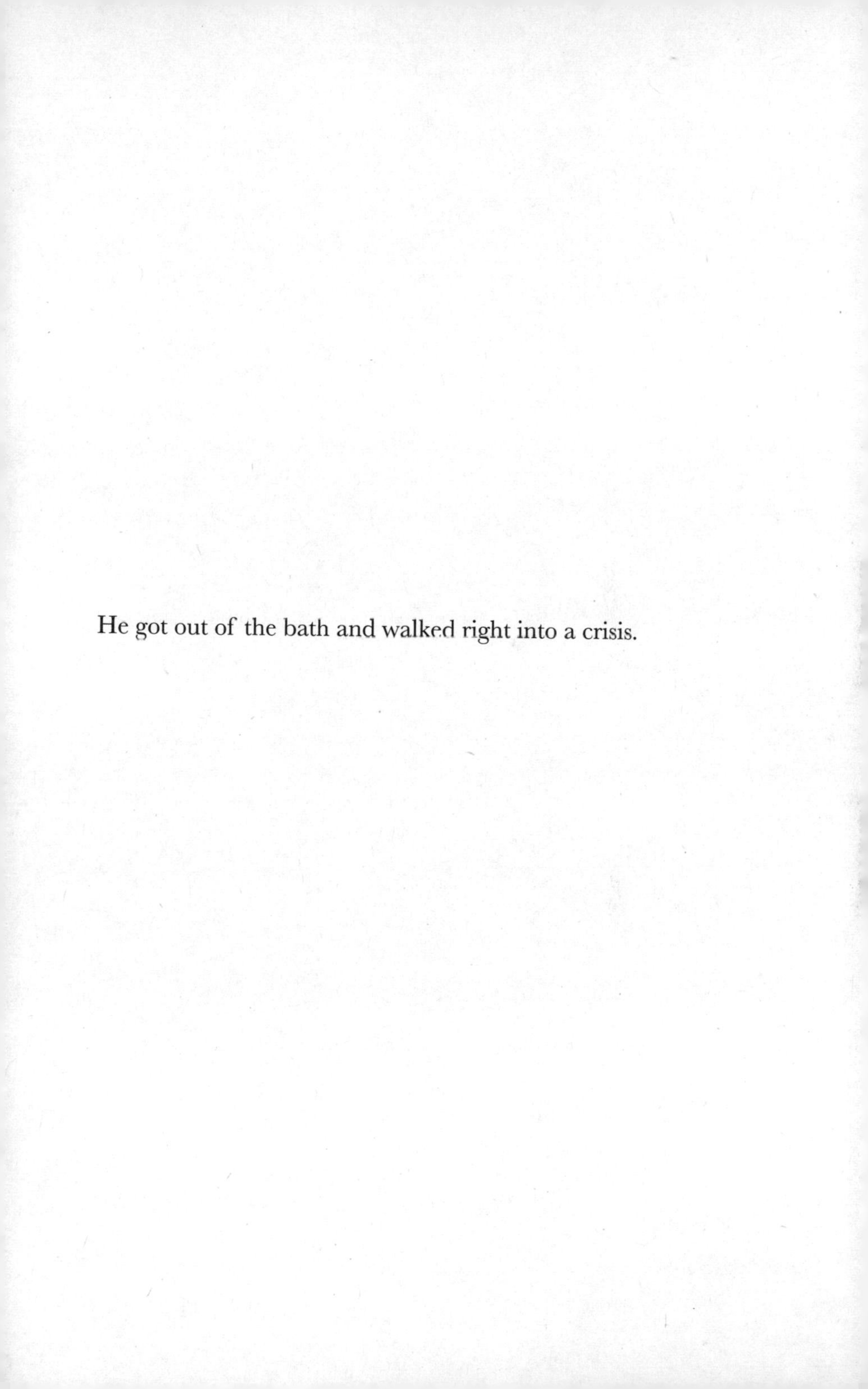
He got out of the bath and walked right into a crisis.

Manifestation of a Girl's Dream

1

This was the greatest peril Sakuta Azusagawa had ever faced.

It was the first day of December, only a month left in the year. A Monday evening, already past ten.

The living room, normally a place to kick back and relax, was currently crackling with an unprecedented level of tension. There was a current running in the air.

They'd taken the *kotatsu* out just yesterday. The heater under the tabletop was on, and everyone's legs were inside the blanket around it, but he couldn't feel a trace of warmth. He considered lying down and pulling himself fully inside, but that wasn't a viable option now. Even stretching out his legs felt risky. No one had specifically demanded it, but Sakuta was on his knees, his back bolt upright, no trace of his usual listless slouch.

It took only one glance around the room to see why.

There were two girls seated at the *kotatsu* with Sakuta.

On his right was an actress, a year above him at his high school. Her name was Mai Sakurajima. She'd been a child star, a household name across Japan. These days, she was filling major roles in TV shows, commercials, even movies—but to Sakuta, she was also his girlfriend. She had beautiful features that left a strong impression. Long, black, glossy hair only enhanced her beauty. She'd come directly from the film set, so her makeup was flawless, and she looked even more grown-up than usual. If the circumstances were less extraordinary, he would've loved to just sit and stare. He was confident he could keep that up for two or three hours without a trace of boredom.

But this wasn't the time.

To his left was another girl, cheerily peeling a tangerine like she had not a care in the world. Her name was Shouko Makinohara. She was none other than Sakuta's first love and appeared to be a college student. Despite the ongoing crisis, she was simply helping herself to some tangerines and muttering, "Wow, that's tart." Did she have nerves of steel? They were in the apartment where Sakuta and his sister lived, but judging by how relaxed she was, it would be easy to confuse this for *her* home.

Both Sakuta and Mai found themselves looking at her expectantly. It wasn't clear if Shouko picked up on that or not, but she popped the last piece of tangerine in her mouth, said, "Let me put the kettle on," and started to get up.

"I'll...," Sakuta began.

"*I'll* do it," Mai said firmly. She was on her feet before either of them could argue.

"No, I should—," he tried.

"Sakuta, you sit right there and figure out a good excuse," she snapped.

He didn't dare argue further.

"Okay. Sorry."

He settled back down. She was already furious, and it would be a truly terrible idea to risk antagonizing her anymore.

Mai moved elegantly over to the kitchen counter. With the relaxed poise you'd expect from a girl used to being in her boyfriend's house, she opened the cabinet doors and pulled out the teapot, mugs, and tea caddy. She got water boiling in the kettle and readied a tray to carry everything.

If only it had been just the two of them, Sakuta could have fully appreciated the blissful sight of his girlfriend making herself at home in his kitchen. But for the first time ever, he found it impossible to savor the moment.

As Mai sprinkled tea leaves into the pot, she glanced at the side of the sink. Sakuta couldn't see it from where he was sitting, but she was probably looking at the drying rack. The dishes he and Shouko had used earlier were drying there.

Crap. A shudder ran down his spine. Every muscle in his body tensed up, and a cold sweat formed on his brow.

Mai put the lid on the caddy and slowly raised her eyes. She scanned the living room with feigned indifference. Her eyes lit on something at the back of the room, and he thought he saw a flicker of a frown. Was something over there incriminating?

Sakuta turned to look and instantly saw the damning circumstantial evidence. It was visible through the big glass doors that led to the balcony. Laundry was hanging on the line outside. Sakuta's T-shirt and underwear sat right alongside Shouko's clothes. At least her underwear was drying in another room, but seeing their clothes hanging together was certainly the sort of thing that invited uncomfortable questions.

It screamed "shacking up together."

Of course, his relationship was Shouko was nothing like what that implied. Shouko might've been his first love, but Mai was his girlfriend, and his life was devoted to her. But this fishy sight roused suspicion that was powerful enough to override anything he said to the contrary.

Letting her examine the room further would only dig his grave deeper. He reflexively started talking. "So, uh, Mai…"

"What?"

She sounded curt. Didn't even glance his way.

"Did the shoot wrap early?"

Mai had gone to Kanazawa for location shooting ten days ago. When she called last night, she'd said she had another three days to go. Had that been a ruse in an attempt to catch him red-handed?

"We're not done yet."

She still wasn't looking at him.

"Is it okay for you to be here?"

"I got an opening in my schedule until tomorrow evening, so I came back to see you. Yet *you* don't seem pleased to see me."

"N-no, I'm delighted. Obviously."

He tried to make it sound natural and nonchalant, but only succeeded in making it sound super fake.

"It sure doesn't look like it."

Her eyes were back on the signs of cohabitation.

"That's not true," he said, hoping to buy himself some time. He had to find something convincing to defend himself. But before the words came to him, Mai returned to the *kotatsu*, carrying a tray with mugs and a pot of tea.

She put a hand on her skirt to keep it in place and sat down gracefully, legs neatly pressed together. With practiced ease, she poured tea into each cup. She filled each one a third of the way up, then made a second pass to get them to half-full. On the third and final pour, she filled them to 80 percent and at last said, "Here you go," before placing one in front of Shouko.

"Thank you," Shouko said, accepting it politely.

"And yours, Sakuta."

"Thank you."

He'd been worried he wouldn't get one, but this fear proved unfounded.

"Have some of these as well."

Mai had taken a package of *manju* out of a souvenir bag and was opening it. The snacks were decorated like rabbits and were quite cute.

"Seems almost a shame to eat them," Shouko said as she reached for one anyway. "Oh, these *are* good!" She smiled happily.

Sakuta tried one, too. But the tension in the air was too great, and it turned to ash in his mouth.

He took a few sips of his tea, not wanting to let it go cold after Mai had gone to the trouble.

Letting out a long breath, he slowly put the mug down on the *kotatsu*.

"Let's start with the most important thing," Mai said, as if she'd been waiting for this cue.

There was a look of deep suspicion in her eyes—directed across the table, at Shouko.

The reason for this required no explanation. Shouko's very existence was inherently suspicious. Both Mai and Sakuta knew another Shouko Makinohara, separate from the one sitting in front of them. They'd met the other Shouko that summer. She was a young girl, in her first year of junior high. They'd found her standing by an abandoned kitten, at a loss as to what to do.

She'd eventually adopted the kitten and named it Hayate.

The two Shoukos looked so much alike that it was stranger to assume they weren't the same person—but there was a significant age difference. One was still a child, in junior high. The other was much older and almost certainly college age.

That posed a huge question, one that had been lurking in the corner of Sakuta's mind since they met the younger Shouko that summer. If they were going to talk about anything, they would have to start by clearing that up. Mai was right. That was important. The most important thing.

"And what might that be?" Shouko asked, hands around her tea mug.

"How long have you two been shacking up together?"

"We aren't!"

Mai's question surprised him, and he issued a cry of denial before he could stop himself.

"Fine, 'living together.'"

"It's not a semantic issue. Also, is that really the 'most' important question?"

He'd been so sure she would ask about what was going on with Shouko herself.

"Nothing could be more important."

"Well, I for one thought there was something else more pressing..."

Sakuta and Mai clearly had different priorities.

"So? How long?"

She was not dropping this line of questioning. There was a quiet power behind her voice. It had not faltered at all, despite Sakuta's best efforts.

His eyes wavered.

"Uh...maybe yesterday?"

Obfuscating seemed best. If he took evasive maneuvers for the moment, maybe he'd buy himself enough time to think of a decent response. At least, that was the plan.

"That's not true, Sakuta. I've been here since Thursday."

How fast his faint hopes were dashed.

Thursday, Friday, Saturday, Sunday, Monday... Shouko was counting on her fingers.

"So we've been shacking up together for five days now."

"Please stop using that phrase..."

It was an important distinction. Maybe nobody else cared, but it mattered to him.

"Would calling it 'five days living together' be better?"

"Can we drop the joke?" Mai asked. No trace of a smile. Her glare was powerful enough to stop anyone in their tracks.

"But repetition is the key to comedy." Shouko said, smiling as if she hadn't noticed.

Sakuta didn't dare look at Mai.

"I mean...Thursday just worked out that way. It wasn't until Friday that you actually asked to stay here."

What was he even saying? Reducing the stay by a single day was not going to help him at this point. He knew it was futile. He just couldn't stop himself from clutching at straws.

"Thursday...was the day Kaede got her memories back?"

"Huh? Uh...yes."

Kaede was Sakuta's little sister. Some trouble with bullies two years ago had caused a dissociative disorder, and she'd lost all memories of the life she'd lived. It was like she'd locked herself inside a shell to protect herself from torment. To distinguish the new Kaede from the original, they'd written her name in hiragana instead of kanji. And hiragana Kaede had lived here with Sakuta.

But last Thursday, she'd gone back to normal. The dissociative disorder had gone away, and the old Kaede's memories and personality returned. Replacing the new Kaede entirely.

"I see…," Mai said softly. There was emotion in her response, a hint of something important, but Sakuta couldn't identify it. She might've been thinking of the Kaede they'd lost, but the way she stared down at her hands suggested there was probably more to it than that. He just couldn't tell what.

"Um, please don't blame Sakuta for all this," Shouko requested when nothing was forthcoming from Mai. "It's not his fault. I'm the one who had nowhere else to go and asked if I could stay here."

"Then you'll stay with me from now on," Mai said, looking up. But only her eyes moved. Her expression didn't change at all.

"Don't worry—we aren't doing anything naughty."

"There's no guarantee you won't," Mai replied, as if discussing a business deal.

"Sakuta would never be tempted to do anything with me as long as his relationship with you is keeping him satisfied."

No matter what Mai did, Shouko's tone never changed. She clearly knew exactly what was going on, but everything she said completely ignored the delicate situation. Sakuta even got the sense she was enjoying this. And he didn't think that was his imagination. Shouko was obviously winding Mai up, deliberately acting like a remorseless home-wrecker. He had no clue what good that did anyone…

But it was definitely wreaking havoc on his stomach.

"I'm keeping him satisfied," Mai said, not quite at full volume. Her eyes were locked on the tangerines in the center of the *kotatsu*.

"Is she, Sakuta?" Shouko asked, turning to him at the worst possible

moment. Specifically because it *was* the worst moment. The Shouko he'd known had been a massive tease like that. This time, it might well end up being worse than "teasing."

And as if intent on driving the final nail in his coffin, Shouko reached under the *kotatsu* and put her hand on Sakuta's thigh.

"Well?" she asked, rubbing his leg.

"Yeeagh!" he yelped as a shiver ran down his spine.

Mai frowned at him. But then her eyes narrowed, and *she* reached under the *kotatsu*, too.

"Eep!"

She'd pinched his thigh.

"You're satisfied, right?" Mai snapped.

"Yes, of course!"

"Then me staying here is no cause for concern and poses no problem."

Shouko smiled like she'd just won this conversation. The whole thing had been a trap, setting up this exact response from each of them.

"Well...," Mai began, but she seemed to have no follow-up. She met Shouko's gaze and held it but was clearly at a loss. Sakuta felt pretty sure he'd never seen Mai so thoroughly defeated. She was usually the one in the lead, keeping everyone under her thumb.

"S-some things just aren't okay," Mai managed to get out at last. It wasn't often she just abandoned logic like that. She was evidently struggling to maintain her usual composure when dealing with Shouko.

"But living together should be totally fine."

"It absolutely is not."

"Even if something *did* happen, that wouldn't be a problem."

Shouko's grin got extra mischievous.

"On what basis?"

"I'm in love with Sakuta."

"Pffff!"

Sakuta had *just* taken a sip of tea. It went everywhere. He coughed pretty hard.

"Look at this mess you made." Shouko groaned, wiping the *kotatsu* down with a tissue. She gave his back a few pats.

Mai's glare was like daggers. Quiet and cold. This was not simple irritation or anger, so he couldn't get a read on it. All he knew was that she was being very intense, and it was crushing him. Maybe this was what Mai was like when she was *truly* mad. The thought was terrifying.

"O-okay, time-out!"

He couldn't stand it any longer and ejected himself from the *kotatsu*. He went straight for the telephone. Before anyone could say a word, he lifted the receiver and dialed.

This was the cell phone number of one of his few friends, Rio Futaba. He knew the full eleven digits by heart. She answered on the third ring.

"What?"

Curt. Very Rio. That was a relief.

"Please help me," he begged in English.

"Who might this be?"

"Azusagawa."

"I knew that already."

"Then why'd you ask?"

"So? What is it?"

"Shouko came back."

"You're having an affair?"

It didn't sound like she was joking.

"She's in my house right now."

"Then I just have to e-mail that fact to Sakurajima."

"Mai's also here."

The moment she understood the situation, the line went dead. She'd hung up on him.

He hit redial.

"What?" she demanded, as if this were the last conversation she wanted to take part in.

"Why'd you hang up?!"

"My capacity for caring cut out."

"What an amazing expression."

"I'm expressing a profound desire not to get mixed up in your ongoing crisis."

"I figured as much."

Sakuta would have been tempted to hang up if a friend called him about this, too. He probably would have done exactly that.

"But I need help."

"Absolutely not."

"Is that any way to be a friend?"

"If you thought of me as a friend, you wouldn't bother me with your drama."

"I'm coming to pick you up right now. Please mediate."

"No need."

"Nah, it's late. Let me bring you over."

"I meant I don't want to go."

"I'm begging you here."

"*Argh*..."

There was a *very* long sigh. No doubt it was deliberately drawn out for his benefit.

"Fine. My mom's about to drive to Narita. I'll have her drop me at your place."

"Seriously, you're a lifesaver."

"Just to be clear, I'm only helping with Shouko's...Adolescence Syndrome. I'm not touching your infidelity with a ten-foot pole."

"...I'll do what I can on that front."

"Later."

He waited till she hung up before putting the receiver down. Letting out a sigh of relief, he turned back to the world's frostiest *kotatsu*.

Rio arrived twenty minutes later, took one look at the living room, and said, "Can I go home?"

She clearly meant it.

Sakuta put his hands on her back and gently guided her over to the *kotatsu*. This was the first time Rio had met the older Shouko.

"She does look exactly the same except grown up."

"I appreciate you coming all this way," Shouko said, bowing her head.

"Now that Futaba's here, will you please explain yourself, Shouko?"

Who was she? What was her connection to the younger Makinohara? He'd been wondering that since summer and would finally have an answer.

"Time to pay the piper, huh?" Shouko said, sitting up. "The simple truth is..."

She broke off and looked gravely at Sakuta, then Mai, then Rio.

"Sometimes I get bigger," she said. Utterly serious.

"......"

"......"

"......"

All three of them said nothing. Just stared at her. Nobody seemed especially surprised or upset by her shocking pronouncement. It was like they'd all suspected as much.

"Sometimes I get bigger," Shouko said again, like she'd expected more of a reaction.

"......"

Still no response.

"Are you even listening?"

"Sure," Sakuta said.

"Do you understand me?"

"We do." Rio nodded.

"Adolescence Syndrome takes many forms," Mai muttered.

"If you aren't even a *bit* surprised, I wasted a *lot* of time dragging this out," Shouko complained.

"Any clue why this happens?" Sakuta asked, moving right along.

"This is really anticlimactic." She looked despondent.

He wasn't about to let her wriggle out of this. He had to extract the full truth from her today.

"It's your fault for making a huge deal out of nothing," he said.

"I think getting bigger sometimes is a pretty big deal!"

"Is this related to your condition?" he asked, ignoring her protests. If he let his guard down for a second, they'd wind up on an endless tangent.

"Probably," Shouko admitted. She glanced at Mai and Rio. They both caught her meaning and nodded. They'd been informed about it.

Shouko had a serious heart condition. The doctors had explained that without a transplant, she was unlikely to survive junior high. That was a lot for any girl her age to handle. There was no way she wouldn't be worried about it. It seemed likely that each passing day was just another reminder that time was running out, leaving her screaming silently each time the sun rose. And if that couldn't touch off a case of Adolescence Syndrome, what could?

A life-threatening illness was a *very* credible trigger.

"To me, it was always a dream."

She picked up a tangerine, but instead of peeling it, she rolled it around in her hands.

"Growing up, I mean." She paused, then continued. "When the doctors said my chances of graduating junior high weren't great... well, ever since the meaning of that sank in, I've wanted to be a high school student. A college student. A grown-up."

She clutched the tangerine tight, like it was something precious.

"The little me knows she can never be any of those things, but she dreams about it. And I think that's what you see here."

Nobody said anything for a while. Everyone was ruminating over what her words meant.

Sakuta was the first to break the silence.

"Can I ask one thing?"

"Yes. Go ahead."

"All of that makes a *ton* of sense, but..."

He trailed off, giving her a look.

"Yes?"

"I feel like you and her are really different."

"Are we?"

"You're much more shameless."

The younger Shouko was modest, sincere, and generally a really nice kid. Definitely didn't have the nerves to wrap Mai around her finger.

"*I'm* the shameless one? Sakuta, you've got three girls sharing a *kotatsu* with you."

"Case in point…"

"Well, blame the other me, then. I'm just the ideal she wishes she could become in the future."

Rio jumped in there. "So can we assume the little Shouko doesn't know about you?"

She seemed convinced she already had the answer to this and was just making sure. Like it was important to confirm this fact. Sakuta had a pretty good idea why she'd asked that.

Sakuta had first met the older Shouko two years ago. But when he'd met the younger one this year, she'd had no memories of him. She'd acted like she was meeting a stranger.

If she was aware that she got bigger sometimes, it would have shown. She didn't seem like the kind of girl who could hide something like that.

"How'd you handle the change before?"

"I didn't."

"Huh?"

"By the time I noticed, I was just suddenly back to normal."

"Didn't your family notice? It went on for days, right?"

No matter where she hid herself, if their sickly daughter disappeared without warning, most parents would call the police for help. And this time she'd been staying with Sakuta for five whole days. It seemed likely the police would be looking for her by now.

"Oh, that isn't a concern," Shouko said firmly.

"On what basis?"

"When I said I get bigger sometimes, that wasn't quite right. While I'm over here being big, little me still exists."

"I've heard of a similar case," Sakuta said, looking across the table at Rio. A single person turning into two. He'd encountered that exact situation before. It was the Adolescence Syndrome phenomenon that had affected Rio. But in that case, they'd both been the same age.

"I've never met the little me, but I was worried about that, too, so I went to my house this afternoon. And my mom was just leaving, so I followed her…and she went right to the hospital where they're treating me. I think my other self is staying there right now. Which is probably why she didn't pick up when you called."

"I see…"

Sakuta had tried to get little Shouko on the phone several times with no success. And she hadn't called him back. If she was hospitalized, that would explain it.

"Then I guess we have a working answer."

"Yeah."

If this Shouko was a dream little Shouko had of the future, then maybe talking to the younger Shouko would clue them in to why this was happening.

"I've gotta check up on Kaede anyway, so I'll stop in to see her tomorrow."

The hospital taking care of Shouko was the same one where Kaede was staying.

Rio rose silently to her feet.

"Bathroom?"

"No. I'm going home."

"Why?"

"The conversation's over, and I'm no longer needed here."

"Stay the night."

"Azusagawa."

"What?"

"You're a creep."

"You're just going to abandon me in this mess?! How heartless can you be?!"

This approach got him nowhere.

"Futaba, sorry. But I'd also like you to stay."

Mai backing him up was unexpected. She hadn't said a word the whole time they were talking to Shouko, and it felt like a really long time since he'd heard her voice.

"I'm staying over tonight, so please join us."

"......"

Rio must not have expected this from Mai, either. She looked genuinely surprised. Less by the request itself than by the fact that there had been a request at all.

"Well, if you insist..."

She settled back down at the *kotatsu*.

"So you'll listen if Mai asks."

"*You* always ask too much."

"I'm unable to live without help from those around me. I'm sure it'll happen again."

As he spoke, Mai got up.

"I'm going to swing by my place, take a bath, and change," she explained before he could ask.

"I'll walk you over."

"No need. It's not that far."

This was true. Mai's condo was in the building across the street.

"Shouko, Futaba, sorry, but I'll leave you here a bit."

"Roger, roger."

At the door, Mai said, "Seriously, you don't have to."

"Gimme a chance to talk to you."

"......"

Mai said nothing more. Just walked out the door. He decided the lack of a refusal meant she'd granted him an audience. He quickly put his shoes on and caught up with her waiting for the elevator. They stood side by side watching the floor lights blink. He hoped it would take its time.

"So, Mai," he began.

"Sakuta," she interrupted. Her voice carried.

"What?"

"Sorry."

That was unexpected.

"Huh?" he said, confused. He was the one who should be apologizing. Hearing "Sorry" from her just made his mind go blank. He could not come up with a single reason why she'd said that.

"The whole incident with Kaede must have been so hard, and I couldn't be here for you."

"……"

She was staring up at the elevator lights. She looked sad, like she was about to cry. Sakuta leaned toward her and tried to put his arms around her.

But she took a step away, pointedly eluding his grasp. It was awkward.

"I can't," she said. "Not for a while."

She didn't even glance at him. An unmistakable rejection.

Before he could think of any response, there was a *ding*, and the elevator doors opened.

"That's far enough," she said as she stepped into the elevator alone.

Before the doors closed, he managed to say, "I'm sorry, Mai."

That was all he could do.

"I didn't start dating you because I wanted to hear your apologies," she replied.

Then the doors closed, and she was gone.

A short conversation, but it felt like every word had been an arrow to his chest. She was right. They weren't dating to hear each other apologize.

He couldn't argue with that at all.

2

The next day after school, Sakuta was on the train home. A Fujisawa-bound train he'd boarded at Shichirigahama Station.

"The sea is so vast…"

The winter sun was easier on the eyes, giving the ocean a soft glow. The sky had donned a pale blue. The horizon divided one from the other, highlighting the contrast.

This was a single-track local line that ran along Sagami Bay from Fujisawa to Kamakura, but it let him see this glorious view on a daily basis.

On the way home from school, there were often tourists on board. Lately, more of these had been from overseas. Right now, there was a handsome blond dude exclaiming "Amazing!" and taking a ton of pictures.

"The sea really is vast…," he muttered again.

He was having trouble mustering much enthusiasm, amazing view or not.

"Quit audibly attempting to escape reality," Rio growled. They were standing to either side of the same set of doors, but she had kept her eyes locked on the book in her hands since they boarded the train.

"You're supposed to be nice to inconsolable friends."

"This *is* me being nice. I've blown off my club duties to visit this hospital with you."

She sure could've fooled him. And she didn't look up once from her book.

"Plus, you're the one who's apparently been having an affair. The prime suspect is not supposed to be the one getting all depressed."

"Could you not kick me when I'm down?"

Her blows were far too accurate. They stung his ears more than he liked. He couldn't argue with anything she said. But he wasn't capable of stoically enduring this whole mess, either. Mai's rejection had hit him hard, and he was not prepared to take that lying down.

He'd upset Mai before, but nothing like this. Everything else had been on the level of "hurt feelings."

"I hope you can see that my current mood is a wholehearted expression of my regret."

"Rather than seek my approval, you should have gotten up on time and made sure you saw Sakurajima off."

Once again, she'd hit him where it hurt.

"She was already gone when I woke up! Which was definitely bad."

That morning, by the time he had gotten out of bed, Sakuta discovered Mai had already departed for her film shoot in Kanazawa. She'd left a note on the table, just a perfunctory *Heading out.*

No matter how early she was leaving, Mai would usually have dragged him out of bed herself. She would've impishly told him she was doing him a favor, figuring he'd want to give her a goodbye kiss.

The parting note he got instead could not be more removed from such delightful shenanigans. He'd felt a chill run down his spine. Not only had a night's sleep not improved the situation, it had clearly grown actively worse.

"And the fact that Shouko gently woke you up is completely indefensible. Given these facts, I am disinclined to comfort you."

"...I was too upset about Mai to fall asleep."

He had *meant* to see her off. But empty intentions did nobody any good.

Sakuta was pretty sure it had been almost dawn by the time he finally slipped into fitful slumber. Mai must have woken up shortly after and left for Kanazawa.

"Save the excuses for Sakurajima."

"......"

Rio was right once again. She always was. He couldn't argue, so instead he inspected the train interior. There was an ad dangling nearby, inviting everyone to visit the aquarium near Enoshima. It also advertised an illuminated jellyfish show. Seemed like an event to attract the Christmas crowd.

"Just having Shouko stay over might have been forgivable, given the circumstances. Especially right after what happened with Kaede. I think Sakurajima gets that."

"I don't want to make Kaede my excuse."

Sakuta's sister had developed dissociative disorder after a nasty bout of bullying two years ago. This had resulted in the loss of her memories and, with those, her personality. Sakuta had spent two years living with the new Kaede—a completely different person.

But last week, the dissociative disorder symptoms had resolved themselves, and the old Kaede had returned in full. But that meant the new Kaede's memories and personality were gone. Along with the two years they'd spent together. Sakuta knew the time they'd shared would never come back. *Should* never come back. Things had turned out this way because her mental illness had been cured. And *that* was the result of a lot of hard work on new Kaede's part.

But even if he recognized this was a good thing, that didn't help him deal with the loss, and it didn't mean he could simply accept everything automatically.

The suffering it caused him was inevitable. And that pain had reopened the wounds on his chest, wounds inflicted by Adolescence Syndrome. He could still feel the blood on his hands. His chest had hurt, his heart had ached, and sadness had threatened to overwhelm him.

If Shouko had not been there to help him, who knew what might have happened. Maybe he still wouldn't be ready to acknowledge the old Kaede's return. Maybe the scars on his chest would still be throbbing. The cavernous emptiness that had opened up inside him was just that vast.

But even so, Sakuta didn't think it would be right to use that as an excuse. He couldn't, and he didn't want to.

"Just make it up to her."

"How?"

"And do it fast so you quit asking me for advice about it."

"Trust me, I would love nothing more."

But how could he make things the way they used to be? He had no idea.

He looked at Rio for help, but she kept her eyes firmly on her book.

"Is that even any good?"

"Very."

She lifted it so he could read the cover. It was called *Unraveling Superstring Theory*. He couldn't tell if the author thought they were being clever or if the title had just been a happy accident, but either way, it sounded like a dad joke.

"Is superstring theory a metaphor for how Mai's gonna be stringing me along the rest of my life?"

"In your case, sponger theory is more applicable."

"As if that's a real theory."

"If you don't get a job, she really will cut you loose."

"I intend to!"

"Then again, she may dump you before it comes to that."

"Don't jinx me, damn it."

"......"

"Why did you go quiet there?!"

"Do you really need me to explain why she's gonna leave you?"

"...No, I'm well aware."

"Then I won't spell it out."

With that loaded statement, Rio finally glanced up from her book and looked him dead in the eye. Waiting for him to ask.

"Okay, what?" he asked. It felt like there was something he wasn't getting.

"Azusagawa, I think you're misunderstanding something."

"Huh?"

"......"

Rio said nothing more. The train had reached Fujisawa Station, the end of the line. She snapped her book closed and stepped off the car. Sakuta hastily followed her. This was not a conversation they could continue after joining the crowds flowing out the station gates.

But she did give him a hint.

"You don't understand women."

"Uh...well, I *am* a man, so..."

* * *

He thought a lot about what this might mean on the way to the hospital but ultimately didn't get any closer to figuring out what he was missing.

Mai was mad because he'd let Shouko stay with him without consulting her. The cause was clear, the situation simple. What part of that could be misunderstood?

"I am without a whit."

But once they reached the hospital, he didn't have time to ponder it further. He would have to make it his homework.

He and Rio were here to see Shouko.

First thing they did was get her room number from reception.

There were security and privacy regulations, so the staff were limited in what they could share, but since this was the same hospital looking after Kaede, all he had to do was say they knew Shouko, and they happily told him.

"Room 301," he said, rejoining Rio.

"She's really here, then."

He checked the floor map.

"Yep."

Big Shouko had been right.

They took the elevator to the third floor. The corridor had that special hush reserved for floors with inpatients. Time seemed to flow much more slowly than on outpatient floors.

Room 301 was at the end of the hall.

There was a nameplate outside, and it read SHOUKO MAKINOHARA in lovely handwriting.

He knocked twice.

"Come in."

That was definitely Shouko's voice. The little one.

"All right," Sakuta said, and he slid the door open. It was almost silent.

They had come to a private room with a southern view and lots of sunlight.

Shouko was sitting on the bed in the center.

But she'd been busy changing. Her pajama bottoms were half on, and she was kicking her legs to pull the cloth further up. Her thighs had clearly rarely seen the sun and were so pale they were almost blinding. When she raised her hips, he caught a flash of white underwear.

"You're early today, Mom… Wait, what?"

Shouko froze, blinking at him.

"Sakuta?" she said.

"That's my name."

Shouko took a big breath.

Sakuta and Rio quickly wheeled around and went back outside, closing the door behind them.

"Aiiiiieeeeeeee!"

A second later, Shouko's scream shook the room.

He sensed a glare from one side. Rio was looking at him like he was some sort of predator.

"I knocked and got permission to enter!"

He was innocent here.

"If you ever saw me naked, it would be a lifelong trauma."

"She had her pajama top on!"

"And below?"

"She was still pulling those up."

"What color were her panties?"

"If I answer that question, I'll be opening myself up to a world of abuse."

"The fact that you have an answer despite the short time allotted just proves you're the ultimate rascal. Truly, a terror among men."

He was shown no mercy even without offering an answer.

"I-I'm ready now," Shouko said. The door opened a crack, and she peered out at them. Her pajamas were fully on now. She waved Sakuta and Rio in and then said, red-faced, "S-sorry, that was…awkward."

She sat back down on her bed, and Sakuta and Rio took seats to one side, using the stool and a nearby folding chair.

"Well, sorry to just drop in on you like that."

"N-no, I'm sure you're the one who wants to scream. I'm really sorry. B-but what brings you here today?"

She looked directly into Sakuta's eyes, seemingly tense. Like she was hiding something.

"Well, I called to see if you wanted me to bring Hayate over again, but I couldn't get through…so I wondered if you might be here."

"A-ah, sorry. My phone's at home."

As she spoke, she discretely picked her phone up off the bedside table and tried to hide it behind her.

Sakuta shot Rio a glance. Rio nodded. Successful eye contact. Rio took her phone out of her bag and started tapping the screen.

A moment later, a ringtone echoed loudly in the room.

"Augh! Augh!"

Shouko pulled the phone out from its hiding place and quickly tapped the screen, silencing it.

"Um…okay, sorry, that was a lie."

"You thought if you answered my call, I'd realize you were in the hospital and worry."

"Y-yes…"

"If you don't even let me do that much, I'll feel so powerless that it'll crush me."

He made it sound like a joke, but he meant every word. Sakuta couldn't do anything to help her recover, so he at least wanted to be able to worry about her.

"S-sorry."

"I'll never forgive you."

"You won't?!"

Seeing Shouko at a loss, Rio offered some advice.

"There's nothing Azusagawa loves more than getting selfish demands. He'd prefer that over an apology."

"Well put, Futaba."

"R-really? Um, but…"

"Anything you want," Sakuta said.

"Th-then, I'd like you to visit again. When you have time, that is," she said, like this was asking a lot.

"No way."

"You said 'anything'!"

"That's way too much work. I'll just come every day."

"Wuh?" Shouko blinked at him.

"I can't be bothered working out how often is too often or not often enough."

"Oh…thank you!"

"Ah, right. Sometimes I've got a work shift right after school, so I might not make it on those days."

Out of the corner of his eye, he caught someone staring at him. Rio. When he glanced her way, that expression was even drier than her usual one.

"What's with that look?"

"You're just openly flirting with her, and it's appalling."

"He's flirting with me?! I wondered why my heart was beating fast!"

"I'm not flirting with you."

"Oh. Shame."

The older Shouko's very existence was sending shock waves through his life, so he really didn't need Shouko the Younger joining the war.

"Um, Sakuta."

"Mm."

"Speaking of selfish requests, I have something I wanted to talk to you about."

"Go on."

When he nodded, Shouko reached for the side table. She picked up a folded piece of paper lying on top of a pile of textbooks.

"It's about this," she said, holding it up so they could both see.

At the very top, it said *Future Schedule* in a very word-processory font. The name field said *Class 4-1: Shouko Makinohara* in pretty handwriting.

"This is…?"

"Something we did in class in fourth grade."

"I think we did something similar."

It had a list of years, and you filled out each one yourself. The school did this to encourage children to think about their futures...or at least, that was probably the point of the exercise.

Sakuta didn't remember what he'd written. He likely hadn't given it much thought. He probably wrote something about going to a local junior high, graduating, moving on to a local high school, then suddenly landing a ticket to the best college in Japan. After completing higher education, he'd become prime minister and get superrich. Back in elementary school, he hadn't known much about college, and prime minister was the first thing that popped into his head that sounded important. And he'd thought being rich was a good thing, so why not?

Even if Sakuta hadn't written that himself, one or two other boys in class would have.

He'd happily filled out the list of years, no reluctance at all, no concerns about any of it. It had been like a game to him.

But the Future Schedule in front of him was nothing so trivial. It was mostly blank. The list of years went all the way until Shouko turned eighty, but she'd only filled in the first fifth. It stopped at the end of high school. There was nothing after that. A blank space that sent an ominous message.

He didn't have to ask if her illness was the reason for it. Shouko had been born with her condition and spent her whole life painfully aware that doctors had given her dim prospects of surviving junior high.

"......"

And for that reason, Sakuta wasn't sure what he should say.

While all her classmates were cheerfully filling in their plans, what had been going through Shouko's head? Just imagining it made him feel sick. He couldn't stand the thought.

"There were a lot of things I wanted to write," Shouko said. "About being a grown-up and what I'd do then. I wanted to show my parents what I'd be like if I got bigger like everyone else."

"Mm."

"But I couldn't do that in class. If I write my future, the grown-ups around me would get upset."

"......"

"I started figuring that out in first grade. 'Oh,' I thought, 'I can't say things like that.'"

"For example?"

"When I said, 'I want to be a florist when I grow up' my teacher put her hands over her mouth and got all choked up. It was really uncomfortable."

That teacher hadn't meant to hurt her. She was clearly very nice. But because she knew about the heart condition, she'd been unable to hide the emotions Shouko's words had provoked.

"I thought, 'If I fill out this whole sheet, the teacher will get upset again.' So I got stuck. The teacher told me to take my time with it and finish it at home."

"And you've held on to it?"

If the homework was here, that meant she'd never turned it in.

"It was in my desk drawer. I planned to write the rest someday."

Maybe she'd hoped that there would come a point when writing about her future wouldn't be such a big deal.

"I'd take it out sometimes, look it over...and not write anything. I graduated without ever finishing it."

If she was still holding on to it, then she must've regretted not completing it. Perhaps part of her knew that filling out this form would be a major milestone for her. Maybe both of those were true. Sakuta could try to imagine her feelings, but without an illness like hers, there was no way he could ever really know what she was going through. Shouko herself probably didn't know the answer.

"I couldn't even write about graduating from junior high. But..."

She sounded confused. She looked down at the page. Sakuta and Rio had the same expression on their faces. What she said and what was on the page itself didn't match.

"Mm? Then what's this?" Sakuta asked, pointing.

Graduate junior high.

Enter a high school with a view of the sea! (Minegahara High is my first choice!)

Meet the boy I'm destined to be with.

Graduate in good health!

"That's what I wanted to ask about."
"Huh."
"I didn't write this."
"......"
The conversation was not going where he'd expected.
"You didn't...?"
"No. It definitely wasn't me."
Then who did? This was getting spooky.
But he did have an idea who might have done this. The other Shouko. The big one.
Rio seemed to be thinking along similar lines. He'd have to ask her about it later. From what she'd said so far, little Shouko didn't seem to know about the big one. They'd have to think long and hard about whether they should tell her. Little Shouko had enough on her plate dealing with her illness, and she didn't need Adolescence Syndrome piled on top of that.
"Um, Makinohara."
"Yes?"
"Is this what you wanted to write back then?"
He pointed at the high school plans she'd claimed she hadn't written.
"Not quite."
"Meaning?"
"It's more like what I want to write *now*."
"I see. If you were to continue, what would you write next?"

"Um. That would be…"

"It might be the key to solving this mystery. Don't worry, Futaba and I won't get upset."

He glanced sideways. Rio appeared mildly annoyed at being spoken for but didn't seem inclined to correct the statement. She'd have said something otherwise.

"Well, if you insist. First, I'd like to go to college."

Shouko spoke softly, as if weighing her own feelings on the matter.

"And I think it would be lovely if I could find a nice boyfriend."

She looked away, slightly embarrassed.

"And once we get closer, we could live together."

"Even as students?"

"Yes. And if that leads to marriage, even better."

"…A very aggressive life plan."

"My mom and dad were married in college. So I always thought that was how everyone did it."

She smiled awkwardly, like she'd worked out since then that it was fairly unusual.

He'd thought they both looked young, but they'd landed each other that early? Maybe Shouko was the reason they'd sealed the deal.

As he thought about that, there was a knock at the door.

"Uh, yes?"

The door opened, and a nurse came in. Shouko's mother was with her. She bobbed her head at them. He'd met both Shouko's parents when they came to collect the cat, Hayate, so they knew who he was.

"Shouko, time for your examination."

"Okay. Um, Sakuta…"

"I'll come again. We'll talk more then."

"Great! I'll be waiting."

Shouko saw them off with a smile, and Sakuta and Rio left her room. They walked to the elevators together.

"What do you think?"

He was asking about the extra entries on the Future Schedule.

"The most obvious answer is that Shouko wrote it herself and forgot."

"A rational theory."

"It's her handwriting and didn't look added after the fact."

The idea had certainly crossed his mind. Those penciled characters looked exactly the same, both the shade and the weight of the lines. If she'd written it on a different day, the pencil would have been sharpened differently, and minor differences would have been apparent.

"The less rational explanation is the older Shouko did it."

"But if that's true…what for?"

"A prank?" Rio shrugged. Didn't sound like she bought that explanation herself.

"Can't exactly laugh that off, though. It *does* seem like something she'd do."

But all that would accomplish was sow the seeds of chaos. Little Shouko had been pretty confused. Who went out of the way to upset themselves? What did that accomplish?

"But we did learn a few things."

"Yeah."

"If we must define the older Shouko's being, we could say she appeared to act out the future little Shouko couldn't write on her Future Schedule."

"Or she's living the future little Shouko might never get to."

"Which matches what big Shouko said in the first place."

——*"The little me knows she can never be any of those things, but she dreams about it. And I think that's what you see here."*

Those words had really stuck with him. A powerful, desperate, unvarnished burst of emotion. You could even call it "a wish." The feelings behind it had a tight grip on his heart.

The elevator arrived. They stepped on board and rode it to the ground floor in silence.

They went back down the same hall they'd come in by.

Sakuta spent the whole time thinking about Shouko's condition. He'd thought he understood how hard it was. He'd felt like he'd wrapped his head around it. But hearing directly from her lips how Shouko felt definitely drove it home and left his head spinning.

She was such a nice kid, trying to go through her life while staying positive, and he wanted to help. But Sakuta had no way of curing her condition. That harsh truth was eating away at him.

There was nothing he could do.

But he wanted to do *something*.

He knew he'd end up doing nothing, and being forced to live with these emotions and that knowledge was extremely frustrating.

"Azusagawa, I think you should just treat her like you always have."

"I know."

It was important to worry. But doing that too much would only make Shouko overly self-conscious about the effect she was having on the people around her, and that would simply increase her problems.

So he had to act like nothing had changed.

"Only other thing you can do is this," Rio said, stopping at the reception desk. She reached for a green leaflet on the counter. A piece of paper, folded in three, with the words *Organ Donor Registration Card* written at the top.

Rio took two and handed him one.

"......"

Sakuta shook his head.

Rio's eyes flashed for a second, but then she understood.

"Oh. You already have one," she said, nodding.

"Got it two months ago."

Right after he found out about Shouko's condition. He'd seen the leaflet at the local convenience store and picked it up. It was already filled out and in his wallet.

Rio put one back and placed the other in her bag.

Naturally, that alone wouldn't save Shouko. It certainly wouldn't make the donor she needed magically appear. It had no real bearing on her personal situation, but if you were hoping for one person's salvation, then becoming a donor just seemed like the right thing to do.

"So what now, Azusagawa?"

"Meaning?"

"You gonna marry Shouko?"

"....."

"I'm sure you're aware the laws of this nation do not allow that until you're eighteen."

"Okay, that's a leap too far."

"You're the one who asked what little Shouko's post–high school plans were. You did that so you could resolve the situation with the older one, right? The extra high school plans included meeting the boy she's destined to be with. That's you, and it already happened two years ago when you met Shouko dressed in her Minegahara uniform."

Rio recited her points too fast for him to interrupt. And everything she said lined up with his conclusions as well.

"It's certainly a distinct possibility."

"And since she achieved that goal, high school Shouko vanished. Or more accurately, her Adolescence Syndrome symptoms subsided."

"So now we've reached the second act, with a college version."

"If her purpose is to achieve the goals little Shouko couldn't write on her Future Schedule, marriage is unavoidable."

"Uh, Futaba..."

Was there no other solution?

"As your friend, I will attend the ceremony. Don't worry."

"Yeah, uh...thanks, I guess."

He decided he wasn't up to arguing the point.

Rio and Sakuta split up at the front doors. He still had to go see Kaede.

On the way back up, he stopped at a vending machine to get something to drink. He had too much on his mind, and all that thinking made him thirsty.

His finger hovered over the button for hot coffee, and then he saw a sports drink next to it. The same one Mai did commercials for. His finger snapped to that instantly.

He downed half the bottle, then put the lid back on. It was too much to chug at once. As he got up from the bench to head to Kaede's room, he heard her voice.

"Oh, Sakuta."

That was definitely his sister's voice. Both new and old Kaede sounded the same, but only one of them still existed.

He turned around and found her coming toward him, slippers flapping. There was a nurse with her.

"If you're in the hospital, why are you hanging out here instead of coming to see me?" she asked, puffing out her cheeks.

"You didn't show up when you usually do, so Kaede has been asking 'Is he here yet?' over and over," the nurse shared.

"I—I didn't do that! I was just wondering aloud about how you were really taking your time."

"And so she came looking for you."

"Just so you know, Sakuta, walking is important for my rehabilitation. They're letting me leave tomorrow."

"You must have been so lonely without your big brother."

"I—I was not!"

Listening to the nurse tease Kaede, Sakuta remembered something else important.

Like she'd said, Kaede was coming home tomorrow. Back to the apartment they lived in. Where Shouko was staying…

He'd been hoping to resolve that situation the night before, but Mai's abrupt return had made everything more complicated.

What would Kaede think if she found an older girl staying with her brother? Especially since Shouko *wasn't* his girlfriend.

"Are you even listening?"

"Uh, sure I am."

"You clearly weren't."

"I'll be here at the usual time tomorrow, so make sure you're ready to go."

"I'm already getting ready. I was packing things up earlier."

She seemed excited about getting out of here.

Sakuta reached an important conclusion.

I'll leave tomorrow to tomorrow.

He was sure his future self would handle it.

For now, he decided to let it be.

He had too much on his mind already, and adding anything else on top might drive him off the deep end.

3

He talked with Kaede until six, when visiting hours ended. Then he walked back to Fujisawa Station. He'd neglected to turn in his shift availability form at the restaurant he worked at.

Normally, even if he forgot, the manager would call him, and he'd just handle it then. But with Shouko staying with him, a lot of problems could happen if the call came while he was out. Best to avert these things before they happened.

But the detour meant he got home later than usual. And all the walking had left his stomach growling. Odds were Shouko would have dinner waiting. She insisted this was a fair exchange for letting her stay with him and had barred him from the kitchen. But that thought just reminded him how angry Mai had been.

"Look, she insisted, all right?"

He felt like offering the excuse even if it wouldn't do him any good.

He got stuck at a red light. While he waited, he looked up at the December night sky, watching thin clouds pass overhead.

There was less than a month left in the year. He couldn't decide if it had been a long year or a short one. A lot had happened, for sure. Meeting Mai. Dating her. Several cases of Adolescence Syndrome. Some of them were even fond memories now.

Maybe next year he'd be looking back at the mess Shouko's appearance had caused in the same way.

But he had some steep hurdles to overcome first. At the very least, he had to find a better solution than the one today's investigation had suggested.

"One that doesn't involve a wedding..."

Midthought, the light turned green. He took a step forward, and a sharp pain shot through his posterior. Someone had just kicked him.

Somewhat belatedly, he turned around, clutching his butt and grumbling, "Ow?"

There was a high school girl standing behind him, in the uniform of a fancy girls' school. A very proper-looking outfit that clashed horribly with her glittering blond hair, which was all piled up to one side. Her conspicuous eye makeup was not the kind of flashy look you applied when your skirt went all the way to your knees.

She was scowling at him, her lips pursed. Looking highly irritated.

When she didn't say anything, Sakuta said, "Sorry, I left my wallet at home."

"Huh?"

"Is this an attempted mugging?"

"Obviously not!"

She tried to kick him again, so he evaded the attack.

"Wait— Waah! Don't dodge!"

The girl lost her balance and apparently blamed him for it.

He knew this girl. Her name was Nodoka Toyohama.

She was Mai's sister from another mother and was currently living with Mai.

"No idol lessons today?"

Nodoka was part of the idol group Sweet Bullet and usually went straight from school to singing or dancing lessons. It was unusual for her to get home this early.

"None of your business."

"Fair."

He didn't actually care, so he just walked away. It would never do to let the light turn red before he crossed.

"Hey, wait up!" Nodoka said, scrambling after him. "We just had a quick meeting today."

She decided to explain herself anyway. And since they lived across the street from each other, they were going the same way.

"......"

"......"

They walked in silence for a while.

The sound of their footsteps echoed and lingered as they crossed street after street.

"Say something!"

"Huh?"

"Also, you walk too fast."

Nodoka grabbed his arm, pulling him back.

"Just so you know, I'm in a hurry to get home. I've got an empty stomach and a full, busy mind."

"You shouldn't be thinking about anything but my sister."

"She *is* what's on my mind."

"Liar."

"I'm being serious here."

"Then what day is it?" Nodoka asked, coming to a halt by the park entrance.

"Huh?"

The sudden, weirdly timed question pulled the rug out from under him.

"Say it." Nodoka's tone was grim, like she was forbidding him from making a joke answer.

"December second. Tuesday."

"My sister's birthday," Nodoka said, before he even finished.

"......"

What had she just said? Birthday? Whose...?

"Oh, shit."

His voice came out in a croak. His mind caught up with his voice a moment later. A wave of panic rushed through him, and his feet grew unsteady.

"You're doomed," Nodoka said, shaking her head. "This is why she came back last night!"

"She didn't say anything!"

"It isn't exactly hard to find out Mai Sakurajima's birthday."

Nodoka took her phone out of her pocket, ran her finger across the screen, and showed Sakuta the site she found.

It was the official site of Mai's agency. Open to Mai Sakurajima's profile page. Which clearly displayed **Birthday: December 2**.

"She should have told me..."

But it was a bit late for that now.

"How could she? You've got your hands full with Kaede. She obviously didn't want to drop this on you, too!"

But that meant Sakuta was supposed to figure it out on his own. According to Nodoka anyway. But he hadn't, so she was mad at him. Furious.

"She's been worried about you and Kaede the whole time she's been on location. She called me every night and only talked about you."

"......"

"But you seemed to be doing weirdly well, and it turns out that's because some other woman was looking after you? Go to hell!"

Nodoka's anger was pretty justifiable.

He was quite mad at himself. This was pathetic. Frustrating. He wanted to go back in time. But that was impossible. He'd just have to do what he could.

"Toyohama."

"Drop dead."

"Lemme borrow your phone first."

"No way."

"It's still December second."

"......"

"Please."

"...Fine. At least wish her a happy birthday."

Nodoka thrust her phone in his direction. She was pissed at him but evidently decided Mai needed this.

He dialed, and the phone picked up on the third ring.

"Azusagawa speaking!" said a cheery woman's voice. It was Shouko's. Naturally—Sakuta had called his own number.

"I told you not to answer the phone, remember?"

If she inadvertently answered a call from his father, it could lead to all kinds of headaches. He'd never hear the end of it. And if his father decided he had to pay a visit in person, it would be even worse. That had to be avoided at all costs.

"You're a bit anal about small stuff, Sakuta."

"No I'm not!"

"Hold on—Sakuta?" Nodoka had worked out he wasn't talking to Mai.

"Just a second," he said, stopping her.

She went quiet and scowled at him.

"So what's up with you?"

"Something came up, and I won't be home tonight. Go on and eat without me. Make sure the windows are locked before bed."

"Got it. Just buy me something in Kanazawa!"

"......"

"Did I guess wrong?"

"No, but...how?"

Shouko ignored this question.

"Have fun!" she said and promptly hung up.

"Whatever. Thanks for the phone," he said, handing it back to Nodoka.

"Are you for real?"

"What?"

"You're going to Kanazawa? Now? You know it's not Kanazawa Ward in Yokohama?"

"Ishikawa Prefecture, right? I can make it if I hop on the Shinkansen. It's only seven."

"Seven forty-five, you mean."

"If it's almost eight, it'll be close."

"Wait, I'll check."

Nodoka quickly started tapping her screen. A few moments later...

"Oh, you're right—you can make it. Catch the Utsunomiya Line at Fujisawa and get off at Omiya. Take the Shinkansen from there, and you'll arrive at eleven thirty-five."

"When's that first train reaching Fujisawa?"

"Seven fifty-five. You got ten minutes."

If he turned back now, he could make it in time.

"I'm off, then."

"Call me when you get there. I'll see if I can subtly pin her location down."

"I don't know your number."

"Gimme your hand, asshole."

Grumbling, she stuck her hand in her bag and felt around. Then she pulled out a pen.

"Come on!"

When he hesitated, she grabbed his hand and wrote on it. It tickled, and he let out a weird noise.

"Seriously, drop dead," she said, like she'd spied some trash in the street.

But she kept writing. Eleven digits. Her phone number.

"That's a permanent marker!"

He rubbed at it, but it wasn't coming off.

"This way, it won't rub off before you get there."

"If I show up with your number on my hand, Mai's gonna be furious."

"You deserve it."

"Right, well. Thanks."

"Just get going, you ass!"

"You're the one who stopped me!" he yelled over his shoulder, already rushing toward the station. He broke into a run to make sure he didn't miss the train. He was soon out of breath. White clouds formed each time he exhaled.

He could leave tomorrow to tomorrow.

But not today.

Today he had to take care of things himself.

So he ran as fast as he could.

4

Having successfully made it onto the 7:55 Utsunomiya Line train, he rode that for an hour and twenty minutes, then got off at Omiya. There, he bought a ticket for the Hokuriku Shinkansen. It was all designated seating, so once on board, he only had to find his seat and wait until he reached Kanazawa.

It was too dark outside to admire much of the passing scenery. He had no one to talk to and had brought nothing to pass the time with, so he was literally just sitting there with nothing to do. Desperate to get there as soon as he could but with no diversions to fill the time, he found it hard to settle down. They were going 160 miles per hour, but he wanted to go even faster.

But regardless of what he wanted, the Hokuriku Shinkansen Kagayaki 519 moved calmly along its route. It stopped at Nagano Station in Nagano Prefecture and Toyama Station in Toyama Prefecture before finally reaching Kanazawa Station in Ishikawa Prefecture exactly as scheduled, at 11:35 PM.

Sakuta was on his feet before it stopped, waiting by the doors. He was on the platform the second they opened.

He headed for the gate, scanning the station for a pay phone. Catching a glimpse of familiar green at the base of the escalators, Sakuta pounced. He dialed the digits on his palm. He must have worked up a sweat, but the Sharpie magic had ensured the numbers weren't even blurred. They'd probably be there all week.

The phone was picked up the second it started ringing.

"Sakuta?" Nodoka's voice.

She'd clearly been waiting for his call. She'd answered way too fast.

"Where's Mai?"

"Where are you?"

"Still inside the Shinkansen gates."

"Perfect. I got a text ten minutes ago saying she's near the roundabout by the station's east entrance. She sent me a picture of a cake the film crew brought in, so I think she'll be hanging around a bit."

"The east entrance, got it. And thanks."

"You don't have much time! Go!"

She hung up.

Sakuta hung up and ran off, following signs for the east entrance.

After he was past the gates, he started searching for the traffic circle in question.

He passed under a dome-like ceiling, all glass and metal frames, and finally made it outside. A cold wind blew through him.

And there was something white in the air. A lot of it.

"You're kidding...," he gasped.

It was straight-up snowing.

There was some torii gate–like art installation outside the station, and the top of it was already covered in a layer of white. The whole thing was lit up and looked magical. He spun around and realized the whole station was beautifully framed by falling snow.

"Kanazawa's amazing," he said, genuinely meaning it.

But he couldn't afford to spend time here. He hadn't come all this way to gawk at the sights.

The bus roundabout was just outside the station, but it was fairly massive. It wouldn't be easy to track someone down here.

But he saw some powerful lights clustered to one side. On stands. And he saw a giant microphone on a rod like a fishing pole. Definitely a film shoot.

There were ropes cordoning off the area, and a crowd gathered outside to watch the filming. Locals and tourists, probably an even split.

As Sakuta got closer, a round of applause went up. The big stars were making their exit. Lots of people were calling out "Nice work" and "Thank you." An older man bowed to the crew and the crowd of fans and stepped onto a microbus. The doors closed, and it drove away.

An instant later, the crowd roared—almost a shriek. A truly stunning actress has emerged from the behind the crew—Mai.

She turned to the staff, politely saying, "Good work today, everyone. I'm looking forward to the final day of shooting tomorrow."

Then a woman Sakuta recognized as her manager led Mai to a white minivan, almost at a run. She turned once before boarding, bowing her head at the crowd of fans.

Sakuta was in that crowd, too, but he couldn't exactly call out to her now. One careless move on his part could cause trouble for her.

The sliding door closed, and the van pulled away. The staff watched it go, and with a sidelong glance their way, Sakuta went after it.

But there was only so far a human could chase a moving vehicle. By the time he turned the first corner, the van was already out of sight.

"Haaah…haaah…"

Panting heavily, he looked right and left, to no avail. Between his emotional state and all the running, he was sweating pretty heavily. He considered taking a gamble and running to the next intersection, hoping they'd be stuck at a light. But he didn't know his way around, and it was nighttime and snowing to boot, so finding a car he'd lost track of once already would take a miracle. And Sakuta knew better than to expect real life to work like a TV show.

His only option was to call Nodoka again and see if she could find out where Mai was staying. But by the time he got there, it would definitely be December 3…and there would be nothing he could do about it.

"I hope she'll be kind and laugh this off as an unavoidable accident…," he muttered. His chuckle sounded hollow.

"It's not even remotely amusing," said a voice behind him.

Sakuta knew that voice. In an instant, his dejection turned into surprise and apprehension.

He swung around, staring in disbelief. She stepped out from behind a building. Wrapped up warm like a prerace marathon runner. It was dark, and her hood was up, so he couldn't make out her face.

"Why did you come here, Sakuta?"

She took another step forward, and the streetlights finally lit up the face of the girl he'd been chasing.

"Mai..." He was genuinely astonished. Why was she here?

"This way," she said. She quickly glanced around them, then grabbed his hand and dragged him into the alley.

Parked on the other end of the backstreet was a white minivan. The same one he'd been chasing.

The back door was standing open, and Sakuta was hastily pushed inside.

"All the way back."

"Right."

He shifted down the seat. Mai climbed in after him and slid the door closed.

The car pulled out. Mai's manager was driving. Ryouko Hanawa, if he remembered her name correctly. Mai had once told him about her old nickname, Holstein.

Mai pulled her hood off, revealing her post-shoot look. She was staring straight ahead, and the makeup brought all her features into sharp focus, making her even more beautiful than usual. This wasn't his Mai—it was the celebrity Mai Sakurajima. The glamorous person on the other side of his TV screen. And that aura made it difficult to talk to her like he usually did.

It didn't seem like she was planning to say anything herself. She was staring at the cars passing them by, looking mildly annoyed.

"......"

"......"

There was a weird tension in the air. An electric energy warning him not to speak.

But Sakuta was in a race against time and couldn't lose his nerve here. The digital clock in the car showed 11:56.

"Mai, when did you notice me?"

She hadn't even glanced in his direction as she left the set. He'd been hidden in the crowd. He found it hard to believe she'd picked him out that fast.

"The uniform really stands out."

He *was* wearing a Minegahara uniform. Spotting that way up here in Kanazawa probably would be pretty noticeable. But in that crowd, it would have been hard to see much of his clothes. And Mai had no way of knowing he'd be in Kanazawa at all.

"Nodoka was being particularly talkative, so I thought there was a chance she'd put you up to this."

"She said she'd subtly get a bead on your location."

The whole plan had been to surprise her and celebrate her birthday. But Mai wasn't surprised, nor did she seem happy to see him.

"Getting up here couldn't have been cheap."

"Well, you're not exactly wrong."

"Do you have the money for the fare home?"

"Maybe if I *don't* take the Shinkansen…"

That was a lie. He'd blown all the money he'd earned waiting tables and, even then, barely had enough to get here. The only way he was getting home involved digging into the money his father wired him and Kaede every month, and that was supposed to cover living expenses. They'd have to be really frugal with their food budget for a while…

He sighed.

"How much do you need?"

Mai clearly knew he was lying. She'd reached out to the seat in front of her and taken her wallet out of her purse.

"…Uh, well…"

He'd made the choice to come all this way, and it didn't feel right to borrow train fare from her.

"Fujisawa to Kanazawa is fifteen thousand yen, I believe," Ryouko mentioned offhand from the driver's seat.

"Then here," Mai said, handing him two ten-thousand-yen notes.

"I promise I'll pay you back."

He felt like he'd never looked more hopeless. He was being a total freeloader. This was on the same level as sponger theory.

"You have a place to stay?" Mai delivered another blow.

"I was gonna kill time somewhere till morning."

"In this snow?"

"......"

Her tone made it clear she wouldn't tolerate arguments or flippant remarks, so he simply shut up. She was definitely treating him like a kid.

"Ryouko, sorry, but can we find him an empty room at the crew hotel?"

"I'll stop the car and call."

"...Thank you," Sakuta said. It seemed like his best option. Trying to turn down the offer would just make things worse.

"So?" Mai sighed, glancing at him. "Nothing else to say for yourself?"

Her eyes flicked toward the clock. 11:59.

"Happy birthday, Mai."

Just as he finished, the digital display clicked over. Midnight. It was officially December 3.

"You said that waaay too late, stupid," Mai said, finally smiling. Her eyes on him.

As the van drove away from the station and the center of town, it slowly climbed a hill, stopping five minutes later.

Ryouko pulled the hand brake, took off her seatbelt, and said, "We're here."

"Thanks, Ryouko."

"You've got fifteen minutes for your date. If more pictures of you two end up in the weeklies, I'll never have the courage to face the president again."

"Don't worry. Nobody will care about a second round."

"Augh, Mai!"

"We'll be careful." Mai replied obediently, like a little kid.

"And have this boyfriend cheer you up properly," Ryouko said. This time the advantage was clearly hers. "You've been gloomy ever since you got back, and the crew and director are all worried."

"R-Ryouko!"

It wasn't often he saw Mai this rattled.

"Don't say stuff like that!" she said. The way her lips jutted out was very childish. Or maybe just…her actual age? Before he knew it, Sakuta was smiling.

"What are you smirking about? Come on."

Mai opened the door and got up. The cold air hit him, and he shivered.

"But Mai, it's seriously cold out there."

"You can borrow this."

Mai took off her down jacket and handed it to him. She was wearing her usual coat underneath, which looked pretty warm.

Mai hopped out, so he put the borrowed down jacket on and followed. He realized the jacket had the movie's title logo on it. They must have had it made for this shoot.

He took a few quick steps through the snow, catching up with Mai. The view in front of him suddenly opened up.

"……"

His jaw dropped. They could see all of Kanazawa from here.

"Ryouko showed me this the first day of filming. Pretty, isn't it?"

"Your manager knows the area well?"

"The boyfriend she almost married is from here."

"That…sounds awkward."

She must have come here to meet his parents. That didn't happen unless you were pretty sure. He didn't know what had gone wrong, but it seemed best not to ask.

"That reminds me, Mai."

"What?"

"You were feeling gloomy?"

"While you seem totally fine."

A devastating counter.

"I was a mess."

Without deflecting with jokes or lies, he shared how he still hadn't gotten over what happened with new Kaede.

"...I should be grateful to Shouko. She's saved you twice."

The first time had been two years ago, when he was still in junior high. He'd met high school Shouko on the beach at Shichirigahama, and she really had saved him. The second time had been last week. When the grief at losing one Kaede had overwhelmed him, she'd shown up to scold him.

"I couldn't be there for you," Mai said. Flattening the emotions in her voice. A trace of sadness appeared on her face.

"Well..."

He started to make excuses for her but...decided not to.

Two years ago, Sakuta and Mai weren't together. They weren't a couple. They hadn't even met yet.

There was no need for her to feel bad about it this time, either. She was playing a lead role in a movie filming here in Kanazawa.

"And I know you needed help from *someone*."

But apparently the way things had turned out didn't seem to sit well with her.

"It's just...it hurt that it wasn't me."

She spoke like she was talking about someone else. Maybe she was. There are times you have feelings that surprise you so much they feel like they aren't even yours. Mai might maintain a mature veneer, but that didn't make her immune to unexpected emotions.

"You being here is all I need to feel happy," he said.

"That's the same as me doing nothing."

"I think that's even more impressive. I wish I could be like that for you."

He gave her a hopeful look. But she very deliberately avoided meeting his eyes. He gave up and kept talking.

"Yesterday…I mean, I guess the day before yesterday now. I was really happy you came back."

"Even though I apparently showed up with some very inconvenient timing."

"I have no words."

He winced. He'd definitely panicked at the time.

"Getting your old flame to comfort you? Who do you think you are?"

"Yeah, Shouko was never like that. You're the only one—"

"I don't believe that for a second."

Mai wasn't even gonna let him finish protesting.

"Aww."

"More importantly, it's freezing out."

Now she was changing the subject. She glared at the down jacket like she wanted it back.

"I got you loud and clear," he said, opening the jacket to take it off. But before he could, Mai slipped inside, pressing her back up against him.

"Close it up! It's freezing."

Her wish was his command.

"I thought you said we couldn't do this for a while."

That rejection had hit him hard. Just remembering it made his heart break.

"It's cold, so we can."

"Hooray for winter."

"And you don't need to keep making excuses."

"I'd still like you to hear them."

"I meant you came to see me, so all's forgiven."

This statement was in a much quieter voice. It sounded like she was mad at him and embarrassed but was trying not to be. From behind, he couldn't see her face. But feeling her this close at hand was all he needed.

"......"

"......"

"Sakuta."

"What?"

"Close your eyes."

"Why?"

"Just do it."

There was a note of urgency, like the shame was catching up to her. Thinking he'd better do what she said, he closed his eyes.

Mai turned so she was standing sideways and put her hand on his cheek. He could hear her breathing. Feel her warmth. Smell...something, maybe her shampoo or her makeup. A tantalizing scent that reached his nose despite the snow.

"Sakuta...," she said sweetly. Tantalizingly.

She held her breath.

He could feel her stretching up.

And just as her weight leaned against him...

"Owww!"

...she twisted his cheek, hard.

His eyes snapped open.

"That hurt, Mai!"

He looked at her for mercy, but she didn't let go.

"Also, why?"

That had seemed like the lead-up to a really nice moment. He'd truly let himself believe a kiss or something equally pleasant was forthcoming. This was a cruel twist.

"I'm annoyed by how relieved I was to see you."

She seemed incredibly upset by this fact.

"And I still haven't punished you for cheating on me."

"I haven't cheated!"

Who was it who said he didn't need to make excuses?

"Oh, but I guess if you were relieved, then it's all— Owww!"

When he tried to change the subject, she twisted his other cheek.

"Sakuta, where's my present?"

"Your what?"

"My birthday present."

"I'm not enough?"

He'd emptied his wallet getting here. The account he kept his work money in was down to a few hundred yen.

"No."

"I'll do something better for Christmas, so let me off this time."

"I don't know what my work plans are then."

"I want to eat cake with you."

"You should really spend it with Kaede this year."

"Christmas with my sister?"

"You do that, and I'll give you a present, too."

She glared up at him through her lashes. This was oddly unscary. Maybe because even in the dim light he could tell her cheeks were red.

"We've been together six months now…and today…well, I want to return the favor."

Her voice was so soft it almost got lost in the wind.

"Mai, is this something sexy?"

"…Couples usually do those things."

"I am aware."

"So don't you go panting after any other women."

Mai was usually so regal, but between the shame and the cold, she seemed smaller. Like a frail thing cradled in his arms. It was adorable, and he was not going to hold himself in check for long. He let the impulse overwhelm him and tightened his arms, pulling her closer.

"H-hey! Sakuta! Not yet!"

"It's your fault for being too cute."

She'd driven him off the deep end.

"H-hey! Where are your hands going?"

"Ow!"

Beet red, her heel scored a direct hit on his foot.

"Owww!"

He was left hopping around on one foot, cradling his wounded limb to his chest.

Mai pulled away and straightened her disheveled hair.

"Ah, Ryouko just texted me," she said as she left him behind. "She found a room for you."

"...Thanks," he gasped, barely able to speak through the pain. He stopped hopping and curled up.

"You're such a ham," she said.

"It really hurt this time," he said, glaring at her boots with tears in his eyes. Those things were deadly weapons.

"Well, you shouldn't have touched me there."

He could still feel the softness on his palm. No matter how cold he got, he'd never forget it.

"Quit fantasizing about it."

"You're a grown-up, Mai. Nothing I can imagine would faze you."

"You're just being gross."

"Aww."

"Oh, and I'm staying at your house until the Shouko thing is resolved."

"So if I never resolve it, you'll never leave?"

They'd yet to figure out a concrete game plan for this Adolescence Syndrome. Well, they did have one idea, but it wasn't a realistic one.

"Sure, but we'll never be alone together. Isn't that a problem for you?"

She smirked at him. That was her old smile. She turned to head back to the car, light on her feet. Just watching her like this made Sakuta feel all right.

Kaede would be coming home tomorrow. Shouko would be there.

And once filming was done, Mai would come rolling in, and it would be pure, unbridled chaos. Just thinking about it gave him an ulcer. But he just had to relax and enjoy it. Life wasn't something you could control.

"I'll leave tomorrow to tomorrow," Sakuta muttered.

But as he climbed in the van, Mai said, "It's already today."

Forcing him back to reality.

Her Future Schedule

1

He knocked twice on the clean white door of the hospital room, and Shouko's cheery voice called, "Come in."

"It's me...Azusagawa."

Last time—yesterday—Shouko had still been changing, so he'd learned from that experience and was making sure she knew who it was. This was all part of growing as a person.

"Oh, Sakuta! Don't worry! My pants are on!"

Sakuta expected one more word, then realized it was *fire* and dismissed that line of thought. Clearly not what Shouko meant.

He opened the door and found her sitting on the bed, holding a volume of manga. The pink logo suggested it was a *shoujo* title.

"......"

Shouko's smile was so innocent it momentarily robbed him of words. Was he imagining it, or did she seem even smaller than yesterday? It had only been twenty-four hours, but she seemed much thinner.

"Sakuta?"

"Uh...am I interrupting?"

He glanced at the manga as he took a seat on the stool by the bed.

"No, I've been waiting for you all day. Today and yesterday!"

She closed the book and set it on the table. The artist's name was Mashiro Shiina. That name sounded familiar. At the culture festival the month before, an attractive woman in her midtwenties had gotten lost on school grounds—and she'd had the same name. Coincidence, or had she been a manga artist? Didn't matter now.

"Brought this for you," he said, handing Shouko a paper bag. She took it but then looked surprised.

"A souvenir?" she asked.

"I just got back from Kanazawa."

"Whaaaat?! How did you have time?! You came to see me just yesterday, right?!"

"I hopped on the last Shinkansen right after and took another back just before noon today."

And came straight from Fujisawa Station to see Shouko, without even stopping at home.

He yawned. He'd figured since he was skipping school anyway, he might as well see the town, but he'd probably overdone it. Mai had said, "If you're in Kanazawa, you should at least see Kenroku-en, Higashi Chaya-gai, and the Samurai District before you go." So he had. He'd decided buses were a luxury and walked everywhere, which had worn him out. But the snow-covered scenery had been well worth the walk.

"You're so grown-up!"

"It was Mai's birthday, so...*yawn*."

He yawned again. He'd napped on the Shinkansen on the way back, but two hours had hardly been enough to catch up on lost sleep.

"That's lovely!"

"It's no big deal."

Shouko seemed so impressed it made him feel guilty. If he'd actually been a proper grown-up, he'd have known Mai's birthday ahead of time and been able to get back on his own without borrowing money from his girlfriend. Or having her arrange a room for him...which she also paid for.

He'd kinda made a mess of things, really. Even the gift he'd brought Shouko was purchased with the change from the train fare, and his next couple paychecks would be spent whittling down his debt.

"Can I look?" Shouko asked, already peering into the bag.

"Of course."

"This is so exciting!"

Eyes gleaming, she pulled out the contents.

The first item was a long thin box. The steamed *manju* inside were decorated to look like bunnies. Same thing Mai had given him the other day. Big Shouko had really enjoyed them, so he'd brought some for little Shouko, too.

The other item was a cylinder—the kind of steel water bottle lots of businesswomen carried around with them these days.

"What's inside?"

The weight of it was a clear indication it was full.

"Open it and see."

"Okay!"

She carefully removed the lid.

"Oh…!"

Shouko knew what it was at once, but she looked so surprised, you could swear she'd never actually seen it before. It just didn't get cold enough where they lived, and it fell only once or twice a year, at best.

"Snow?!" she yelped, touching with her fingers to confirm her suspicions.

He'd filled the flask to the brim with it.

The snow from the night before had kept falling as he slept, and by the time Sakuta had woken up, all of Kanazawa was covered in a white blanket.

At the station souvenir stand, he'd found a steel flask with Mount Utatsu on the side (only sold in Kanazawa!) and decided to fill it with snow to take home. Mount Utatsu was where he and Mai had taken in the night view of the city.

"It's so cold!" Shouko cried. She'd poured some snow onto her palm and was happily patting it into a ball.

Seemed like the snow had lasted pretty well.

"Was there a lot of snow?"

"Like six inches this morning."

"Wow! It didn't snow here at all."

She looked out the window. The sky above was clear and blue. A classic winter day.

"It's just not cold enough yet. Hopefully by Christmas..."

"Christmas! I hope I can go this year."

Staring at the southern sky, Shouko seemed lost in memories.

"To what?"

"Oh, the Enoshima Illumination. My mom and dad took me last year. It was so pretty! All the lights, like a dream!"

Shouko was using her whole body to try to explain how great it was.

"Have you ever seen it, Sakuta?"

"From a distance."

Enoshima had a lighthouse-like building called the Sea Candle, and he knew this time of year it was covered in lights. Recently, it got dark early enough that if he stopped to chat in the science lab, the sun would set, and he could see the lights on Enoshima from the train home.

"But going to see that sort of thing alone is cruel and unusual punishment."

Especially on Christmas. That would be pure hell. Couples everywhere.

"But you have Mai!"

"Her work plans aren't set yet."

He was hoping to spend Christmas with her, but things might not work out that way. She *was* a famous actress.

"She's so busy!"

"And if we go on a date in public, it'll attract a lot of attention. But I'd love to see it once, since we do live in the area."

"Th-then you could go with me!"

"With you?"

"I—I mean, not on Christmas Day or anything. Or...you could take Rio, Kaede, Nodoka..."

Shouko was turning bright red, and her voice gradually dwindled away.

"Yeah, good idea."

"Huh? It is?"

She looked up, a smile blooming like a flower.

"When you get out, we can do that to celebrate."

"Okay! I can't wait." She grinned happily. "Oh, Sakuta…"

"Mm?"

"About the thing from yesterday…"

She put the snow back in the flask, dried her hands with a towel, and held up the homework assignment.

Still mostly blank.

"…Oh."

"Yeah."

He knew what Shouko wanted to say without her explaining anything. It was a simple game of Spot the Difference that anyone could have solved.

"There's more, huh?"

"They're increasing."

Yesterday the entries had ended in high school, and everything after that was blank. He was sure of that. But this time it didn't stop there.

Start college.

Reunite with the boy of destiny.

Tell him how I feel!

All three lines were new.

No difference in handwriting. Didn't even appear to be something added after the fact. They looked like they'd always been there, long before this printout got any wear and tear on it.

But it was the specific contents that concerned Sakuta most.

They were familiar.

He had been reunited with the older Shouko.

And she had actually told him how she felt.

——*"I'm in love with Sakuta."*

Those two points, at least, seemed tied to the older Shouko's actions. Things were turning out just the way Rio had said. The older Shouko had appeared to live out the Future Schedule little Makinohara had not been able to write when she received the assignment. Two years ago, when he'd met high school Shouko, she'd acted out what was written in the corresponding section of the form and vanished. Looked at that way, it *did* explain a lot of things.

But if that was true, then this case of Adolescence Syndrome wouldn't subside until college-aged Shouko filled in all the plans for the college student section of the schedule.

And given Shouko's plans, that could be a problem.

She'd already basically moved in with him, so maybe they could count that wish as granted, but...he couldn't exactly marry her.

"Sakuta?" Shouko said, peering up at him. He'd gone a bit too quiet.

"I'll relay this to Rio," he said.

"Okay. Thank you!"

Her smile seemed so carefree. Even though she must have been anything but. Even though her condition must've been terrifying. Shouko didn't let those feelings show, so Sakuta wouldn't see. She didn't want to worry anyone. To worry him. He knew that desire compelled her to hide her emotions.

And the pressure that built up from doing that was being vented elsewhere. Causing her Adolescence Syndrome.

Sadly enough, that knowledge didn't help him solve the root problem.

He couldn't cure her illness.

Put like that, it was a simple truth...but one that left a deep gouge in his chest.

After that, he and Shouko ate some bunny *manju* together, and when four o'clock rolled around, he left her room with a promise to come again.

It was time to go pick up Kaede. She was getting released today.

As he reached the elevators, the bell rang, and the doors opened.

A woman stepped out. She was in her mid to late thirties. This was Shouko's mom.

"Oh, Azusagawa," she said, bobbing her head.

"I just went to see her," he reported.

"Thanks for doing so much for her."

"Not at all."

"She was so excited that you'd stopped by. Even though she made us promise not to tell you she was here. Oh, the elevator!"

The doors had started to close, so she hit the button to stop them.

"I'll come again," he said and stepped on board. Holding it here any longer would be bad manners.

"Good, she'll be thrilled. Thanks!"

The doors slowly shut. As they did, he thought he saw a shadow pass over Shouko's mom's face, but the doors were closed before he could be sure.

Alone in the elevator, he leaned against the wall, listening to the whirr of the motor.

"Not a good sign," he muttered.

Her condition might be worse than he thought.

When he reached Kaede's room, she was all packed up.

Her extra clothes and the books Sakuta had brought to help kill time were loaded into sturdy paper bags and a single tote bag. The sheets had been peeled off the bed, and the place seemed suddenly barren. A day before, it had felt lived-in, but no longer.

"You're late, Sakuta!"

"I'm exactly on time."

If he'd come here after classes ended, he'd be arriving right about now.

"Where's Dad?"

Release forms and payments required a grown-up. His father was supposed to be leaving work early to handle that stuff today.

"He stopped by this morning and took care of everything then."

"Mm? He did?"

"Something came up this afternoon that meant he had to shuffle his schedule."

"You should have said something."

"I wanted to, so I borrowed his cell phone to call you, but…" She scowled at him, looking grossed out.

The reason for that was obvious. Kaede had called.

Who?

Sakuta.

And Sakuta didn't have a cell phone. So the only way to contact him was to call their home phone. The home where a college girl was staying. And Shouko kept answering the phone no matter how many times he told her not to.

"And someone picked up?"

Her reaction made the answer obvious, but he was clutching at false hope.

"A woman."

He could've guessed, but it still rattled him.

"Just great."

"Damn it, Sakuta. It totally caught me by surprise." Kaede puffed her cheeks out in protest.

"Well, that saves me a little time, I guess. She's staying with us right now. Hope you're cool with that."

"Why would I be?!"

"In the past two years, social mores have gone through a great upheaval. This sort of thing is perfectly acceptable now."

"That is absolutely one hundred percent just you being a double creep."

"Adolescence makes creeps of us all."

"B-but…you *have* a girlfriend?" Kaede said, her voice rising.

"Don't worry. It's all good."

"In what way?!"

"My girlfriend will be staying with us, too."

Sakuta said this like it clinched his argument. He knew this was a lot to drop on Kaede the day she left the hospital, but the situation left him with no choice. Kaede would just have to get used to it.

"Huh?"

Kaede's eyes had gone real wide. Her jaw dropped.

"Your imitation of a dying goldfish is still amazing, Kaede."

"I have *never* imitated— No, wait, *what* did you just say?"

"The dying goldfish?"

"Before that!"

"My girlfriend will be staying with us?"

His girlfriend—Mai—had said she'd come right home as soon as the shoot wrapped, and assuming everything had gone according to schedule, she was probably leaving Kanazawa now.

"……"

Kaede was gaping at him again.

"I am so lost," she croaked.

"So basically, this college girl has been staying with me, and starting tonight, my girlfriend's gonna be staying, too. Simple!"

"There's nothing 'simple' about any part of this insane situation! What in the ever-loving hell?!"

"Calm down before you make yourself faint."

"You could afford to be a little more concerned, you know?"

"Got tired of it."

He certainly had panicked quite a bit back then—well, it was only the night before last. When Mai and Shouko had faced each other down, a whole storm of emotions had run through him, but if he didn't make his peace with it, it would eat him alive.

"Kaede."

"What?"

"This is reality. Just accept it."

"…O-okay. Fine. I'll try."

"Thaaaat's the spirit."

It was incredibly helpful to have such an accommodating sister.

"But I do have one question…"

"Yeah?"

"Your girlfriend."

"Oh, right."

Kaede's eyes suggested she already knew but also couldn't begin to believe it.

"This thing about Mai Sakurajima has *got* to be bullshit," she said. "I know that's what the diary said, but tell me it isn't true. I asked Dad, but he just stared into the distance with a vague smile, so…that can't be real, right?"

There was a weird desperation to her voice.

Sakuta felt like he should really apologize to his father for apparently giving him the thousand-yard stare. It seemed like it was high time to properly introduce Mai to Kaede.

"Well, let's just say you'll figure that out for yourself later. You'll meet her in a matter of hours anyway."

Nobody would ever believe that the famous Mai Sakurajima was dating their brother. He could imagine his reaction if their positions were reversed. If Kaede said she was dating a famous celebrity, he'd assume she was delusional. And strongly recommend she seek the advice of a licensed therapist.

"Well, that takes care of everything I need to say before we get there. Let's go home!"

Sakuta grabbed the bags before this could get dragged out any longer. He headed for the door.

"Oh, wait…Sakuta."

"Steel yourself for this on the way."

"Not that."

"Mm?"

Something in her voice made him turn to look. Kaede was staring at her fingers and fidgeting. She always did this when she was trying to say something and couldn't find the words. Same as she had two years ago.

"Um, so..."

"You have to pee?"

"...I wanted to say sorry."

He could barely hear her. But the emotions behind that were pretty intense. The full weight of the last two years was contained within that *sorry*.

"Don't worry about it."

"You know what I mean?" she asked, forcing herself to meet his eyes. Looking very nervous.

"I figure you're just blaming yourself for everything."

"...Well, it is my fault."

"That's ridiculous."

It wasn't Kaede's fault that the bullies had come after her. Or that she couldn't go to school after that. Or that she'd developed Adolescence Syndrome and a dissociative disorder. Their mother being unable to handle raising a daughter like that and developing her own mental illness wasn't Kaede's fault, either. No longer being able to live with their parents and moving here to Fujisawa...none of that was her responsibility.

"Don't be so full of yourself."

"Whaaa?"

"You did the best you could, and that's all that matters."

"...Huh." She pursed her lips. Didn't seem satisfied.

She apparently wanted to say something else, so he urged her on with a quizzical look.

Very quietly, Kaede said, "You might be a bit cooler now."

"..."

His jaw dropped.

"Th-that was a compliment! Why did your eyes go so dead?!"

"Honestly, hearing that from your sister is kinda unsettling."

"That's legit mean!"

"But I mean, if I turned to you and was like, 'Kaede, you're way cuter—'"

"Creepy," she snapped before he could even finish.

"See what I mean? Now let's go."

This time, they actually left.

"Oh, wait, wait." She came running down the hall after him and moved to his side. "Thanks, Sakuta. You've really been here for me."

"Kaede, grab one of these bags."

"What, are you embarrassed?"

"No, they're just heavy."

"You're so weak…"

But she took the tote bag from him.

And he put his now freed hand on her head.

"Wh-what?"

"I oughtta be thanking you."

"Huh? For what?"

If Sakuta actually was more admirable now, that was because of what he'd experienced over the last two years. Sakuta knew he was only like this because of what the two Kaedes had given him. So…

"Thank you."

"I'm so lost."

"That's fine with me."

"Ewww."

Still bickering, they left the hospital together. They carried on like that the whole way home, without ever getting bored.

2

The day after Kaede's release from the hospital, Sakuta was gently shaken from his slumber by his girlfriend.

"It's morning. Wake up."

"Mm…," he grumbled, one foot still in his dreams. Sensation gradually returned to his body. His back and hips hurt. This wasn't what his bed felt like. It was too hard. He was lying not on his bed, but inside the *kotatsu* in the living room. His arms and legs were all pulled inside like a turtle.

Even as sleepy as he was, he soon remembered why.

After much discussion, Mai and Shouko were sharing Sakuta's room. They'd laid out an extra futon in there.

"Come on! Up!" Mai said, shaking him again.

"I think it'll take a kiss to get me up," he said, figuring this was the perfect moment.

"Oh? Then I guess I'll just go to school without you."

Sadly, Mai wasn't playing that game. He'd been hoping she'd at least threaten to step on him. Step on him hard.

"Then I'll handle morning kiss duties!" said a voice in his other ear. Even with his eyes closed, he could tell she was leaning over him. A shadow fell over his face, and he could feel her heat.

The only person who would pull a stunt like this was Shouko. Big Shouko.

"Nope, not happening."

Sakuta cracked his eyes just in time to see Mai fending her off. They were sitting on their knees on either side of where his head was sticking out of the *kotatsu*. Mai on his right, Shouko on his left.

"We discussed this yesterday," Shouko said serenely. "And you approved of our shacking up together."

She wasn't technically wrong. They had deliberated the matter in depth. Sakuta had started by explaining the Future Schedule little Shouko had told him about, and he'd sought opinions on how to proceed from there.

They started talking at ten after Kaede went to bed, and the negotiation lasted until three AM. Like Shouko had predicted, in the end Mai folded. "Fine, I'll allow this cohabitation," she'd said. "But as for everything else, let's see how things go first."

She'd made that decision in the hopes of resolving little Shouko's Adolescence Syndrome. The supernatural phenomenon had assumed an unusual form, but given the severity of Shouko's condition, Mai wanted to help her older counterpart live a little when she could. Sakuta felt the same way.

"Cohabitation is the limit of what I'll allow."

"Men and women shacking up together should be allowed to kiss," Shouko insisted.

This seemed like a reasonable argument at first blush, but he was amazed she had the nerve to make it. Nerves of steel.

"Well, ordinarily...," Mai said, unable to find a convincing counterpoint.

"Then we're in agreement! Wake-up kisses are allowed!"

Shouko leaned in to kiss him again, but before she could...

"Then I'll take care of *that*," Mai blurted. She'd turned bright red. Anger, shame, or perhaps frustration? Maybe all at once.

The last few days had shown him a lot of new sides to Mai. He was thinking *My girlfriend's so cute* when their eyes met.

"......"

"......Sakuta?"

He quietly closed his eyes. Acting like he'd been asleep the whole time. He was soon slapped lightly for his troubles.

"Ow."

"So you've been awake."

"I'll be asleep again in a second, just you wait."

"No going back to bed!"

There was another slap, slightly harder.

"Gah!"

"I *will* get mad," she growled.

He froze.

"Right, sorry."

He pulled himself out from under the *kotatsu* and sat up. His back and hips hurt. Shoulders and neck stiff. His whole body was creaking.

He felt really tired.

"Sakuta, your face is pretty red."

"Now that you mention it..."

Mai leaned in from the right and Shouko from the left.

"Are you getting sick?" Mai asked, putting her hand on his forehead. "You've got a fever." She sounded concerned.

"He does?"

When Mai removed her hand, Shouko leaned forward and put her forehead on his.

"Sh-Shouko!" Mai protested.

"Oh, he does!" Shouko said, like there was nothing out of the ordinary.

"Argh," Mai said.

Shouko pretended not to notice her glare. "That's what you get for sleeping in the *kotatsu*," she chided.

Who was it who decided to move in and force him to sleep here?

"I would have been happy to share a futon with you," she said, sulking like this was *his* fault.

As if he could do that with Mai here. Or even without Mai here.

His own breath felt hot. All this aching wasn't just because of how hard the *kotatsu* pad was. He did feel pretty sick. Sitting up had made the fatigue he felt much more obvious.

"It wasn't a dream...," said someone behind him.

He turned his head to look and found Kaede standing in her doorway.

"Morning, Kaede."

"Good morning."

Mai and Shouko spoke at the same time.

"...M-morning," Kaede said, clinging to her door, still in her pajamas. Despite her evident dismay, she managed to greet them both, clearly driven by a desire to do things properly.

But she didn't manage to keep that up for long. Her eyes quickly turned to Sakuta for help.

"Mornin', Kaede."

"Yeah, mornin'."

Sakuta's head wasn't working, and he couldn't think of anything else to do. He wasn't being the most supportive brother right now.

"You're not making it to school today."

"Yeah…"

His voice sounded far away. Like it wasn't coming from the usual place. He knew that was nonsense, but it felt as if he were talking with his ears. He didn't want to turn into that nightmarish creature.

"…Right, on your feet. If you're gonna sleep all day, you'd better do it in bed."

Somehow he managed to get up on his own. It felt like he was about to float away, and he was very unsteady on his feet. But this was his home, and he wasn't getting lost here.

One hand on the wall, he stepped through the door to his room.

"Oh, wait, Sakuta," Mai said, stopping him. But he couldn't stay standing a moment longer and fell face-first onto the bed. He burrowed under the covers, and it felt warm and smelled good.

"Let me change the sheets and pillowcases real quick," Mai said, trying to pull him up.

But he was done moving.

"It's warm, so I'm good. Plus it smells nice," he muttered.

He thought he felt something hit the back of his head, but he was so sleepy he forgot it immediately.

"Don't be weird!"

Even as his consciousness faded, he was aware that Mai had been sleeping here not long ago. But his mind didn't move beyond that thought. He just wanted to close his eyes, stop feeling or hearing anything, and escape this awful sensation as soon as he could.

When his eyes opened again, his bedroom ceiling was staring down at him.

The sun was glowing brightly behind the curtains, but with the lights in the room off, all the colors in the room were washed out like it was evening.

He looked at his clock; it was just past one PM. The special quiet of a weekday afternoon. Schools of all levels were still in session, and the residential areas were at their lowest ebb, population-wise. Being at home this time of day was almost unnerving.

His body still felt like lead, but he was awake.

The door slowly swung open.

"Oh, did I wake you?" Shouko asked, peering in. She opened the door just far enough for her to enter and slipped in around it. Then she closed the door behind her.

"I was up already."

"How do you feel?"

"Extremely crappy."

"If you've got that much pep in you, you're doing a lot better."

Smiling, she came over and sat down on the edge of the bed.

"Is Mai…?"

"I knew you'd ask that first."

"She went to school?" he asked, not taking the bait.

"She considered staying home to look after you but left in time to still make her classes."

"Okay. Good. And Kaede?"

"Worried about you."

"So dramatic."

It was just a regular cold.

"You've got two girls staying here, so her concern is natural."

"Oh, *that*…"

That was concerning. He was certainly concerned about it.

"She's playing with Nasuno right now. We washed her this morning."

"Yeah, I hadn't given her a bath in a while…"

Their cat had probably developed a bit of a wild animal smell.

"Don't worry; she's sparkling now. Thanks to the patented Sakuta-style cat-washing technique."

"The what?"

"When we found Hayate, you taught me how to bathe cats, remember?"

"Oh…"

Earlier this summer, Sakuta had been looking after Hayate for little Shouko, and she'd come over a lot. He'd taught her how to feed and clean him.

But those lessons had all been for little Shouko, and it felt weird hearing about them from big Shouko.

On some level, he knew intellectually that they were the same person, but it was hard for Sakuta to think of them that way.

His relationship with little Shouko had started that summer, but he'd first met big Shouko two years ago. Those first encounters were separate events in his mind, and even trying to consciously draw a line between them was proving challenging.

And there was still a lot about big Shouko that remained unclear. Maybe this was the time to ask.

"Shouko."

"What?"

She turned her head, looking down at him.

"Something I've been meaning to ask..."

A question he'd left unspoken since they were reunited.

"My measurements?"

"Numbers are irrelevant."

"So you prioritize shape and feel? You never let me down, Sakuta."

Why did she sound impressed? He wasn't feeling well enough to banter with her like this, so he got right to the point.

"Shouko, are you the same Shouko I met on the beach at Shichirigahama two years ago?"

"......"

She didn't answer. Just stared at him.

"Are you the Shouko I fell in love with that day?" he asked, trying a different tactic. This one she couldn't run away from.

A smile appeared on her lips. "You were consistently unpleasant."

"Yeah, some total stranger just starts sticking their nose in your business, you're gonna push back."

"And you grew up to be such a cynic. Maybe I gave you the wrong advice."

"Nah, I turned out fine. You did good."

"Clearly not."

"Shouko."

"Go on now, back to sleep."

She got up.

"Thanks for everything you did back then."

"……"

"You really saved me, Shouko."

She turned back, smiled, and said, "Good night."

He closed his eyes again. The sandman had let him have a few wakeful moments but had come back with a vengeance.

As he drifted back to the land of dreams, he heard a voice say, "You're the one who saved me, Sakuta."

But his consciousness was slipping away, and he couldn't be sure if this was real or just a dream.

The next time Sakuta woke, his room was completely dark. No sunlight through the curtains, but he could see light spilling under his doorway from the hall.

There was someone in the darkness with him, sitting on the bed.

"Shouko?"

"Sorry. Just me."

That wasn't Shouko's voice. As his eyes adjusted to the darkness, he could see Mai looking cross.

"Uh…"

"Save the excuses for when you're better. Shouko's been looking after you all day, right?"

"Not really. I slept through most of it."

Facts didn't matter much here.

"You feeling better?" Mai asked, reaching for his forehead. He probably still had a fever. Her hand felt cold. "It's lower than this morning anyway."

Mai put her hand on her own forehead, comparing the two sensations. That was kinda cute.

"You definitely can't take a bath, but what about a change of clothes?"

"Too much hassle..."

He tried to wave her off, but Mai got up, turned on the lights, and opened the closet.

She grabbed a shirt and came back to the bed.

"At least change your top. I'll help."

"I can manage. I don't want you catching this."

He put out a hand to stop her, but she just said, "No."

"Huh?"

"Let me act like your girlfriend here," she said, a touch of sulk to her tone.

"You always do."

"Like when?"

"When you step on my foot."

"......"

That was clearly the wrong answer. Her eyes took on a dangerous gleam. She was *definitely* going to help him change now. As proof, she'd already grabbed the sleeve of his pajamas.

"Hands up."

Deciding resistance was futile, Sakuta raised his arms as ordered. She pulled on the shirt and peeled it off him.

He was definitely still sick. The air hit his bare skin and made him shiver.

"Sakuta, your..."

As she folded the used shirt, Mai was looking at his chest. She sounded surprised and worried.

Her eyes were locked on the three claw marks carved into his chest. What had previously looked like old scars were now the color of blood. Like a solidified hemorrhage.

"Uh..."

Sakuta briefly debated trying to lie about it, but when his eyes met Mai's, he immediately abandoned the idea. He figured the best way to avoid worrying her was to confess what little he did know.

"The day everything with Kaede went down, they started bleeding again...and now they look like this."

These scars seemed to reflect the pain in his heart. They'd first appeared two years ago, a result of his regrets over being unable to save his sister when the bullying got so bad that she developed a dissociative disorder. Sakuta felt they were a manifestation of the emotional wounds that had torn his family apart. And something similar had happened last week, when he'd realized new Kaede was really gone.

"Does it hurt?"

"Not now."

It had hurt a lot when it was bleeding. But he hadn't been able to tell if that was the scars themselves or the grief in his heart. Hindsight had not clarified that point.

"And it's Adolescence Syndrome."

"Probably."

"Okay..."

Mai was clearly swallowing her words. He didn't need to ask; he could imagine what she'd almost said. If these wounds were the result of his failure to save Kaede, you'd think they'd have healed up once Kaede came back. But they were still here. And worse than before. This wasn't what new Kaede would have wanted. She'd worked so hard to be his little sister and to make him a great brother who'd made his sister's wishes come true.

"......"

"It takes time," Mai said, seeing him lost in thought. "Scars on the heart don't heal overnight."

"I know. No point in putting on a brave face now."

"Right, hands up again." She was holding out a fresh shirt. She seemed to be enjoying this a fair bit. Apparently, it was rather fun looking after Sakuta.

Sakuta was enjoying it as well, but he could only take this so far.

"I'll do the rest," he said as he took the shirt from her.

"Nope!" she snapped, pulling it back.

"Seriously, I've got it. Thanks, Mai."

"You usually let me spoil you rotten. What's going on?"

"I mean, I would love to, but…"

Not sure what he meant, she gave him a puzzled look.

"You might catch this, miss work, and cause trouble for a lot of people," he said, pulling the shirt on. When his head came out again, her lips were tight. She might've just been angry, he thought, but he could tell that wasn't quite it.

"That's, well…it's true, but…who cares?"

It was like she knew he was right but didn't want to give in, like a kid who wanted to keep playing after being told it's time to stop. It was not at all convincing.

"Mai," he said, pushing back. Sometimes saying someone's name was the best way to stop them.

"I *know*… Why am I the one getting scolded here?"

She shot him a frown, but there was the hint of a smile in her eyes.

"I think that's a first," she said. "I might even like it."

"This gonna be a new thing for us?"

"From time to time." She winked at him. "Get better soon. Exams are next week."

With that, she stood up. All reluctance gone. Back to her usual self.

"Argh, don't remind me."

"Good night," she said, waving as she started to close the door behind her.

"Oh, Mai…"

"What?"

"I could really go for some canned tangerines."

Mai blinked at him a moment, but then she said, "You're such a snot. Fine, I'll go buy some."

And then she really did close the door.

A silence settled over the room. With nobody talking, he could hear the faint sounds of the TV in the living room. Kaede and Shouko must've been watching something. Listening to the faint murmur, Sakuta decided getting sick wasn't all that bad.

3

When he stepped off the train, he could smell the sea.

"Kind of a relief..."

The tiny station was packed with Minegahara students. He'd been in Kanazawa on Wednesday and out sick Thursday—only a two-day absence, but it felt like ages since he'd caught a whiff of the sea breeze sweeping in from Shichirigahama.

It was Friday, December 5.

Sakuta had considered using his illness as an excuse to cut straight to the weekend and not go back until Monday, but when he'd woken up that morning, he was in perfect health. He'd tried pretending he still had a fever, but Mai saw through the lie immediately.

"You're a lousy actor. If you're feeling better, get some clothes on."

Mai Sakurajima had been a genuine talent since early childhood, and her evaluations were not to be argued with. His only option was to apologize and do as he was told.

He joined the line of students putting their train passes through the gate and left the station. Everyone wearing the same uniform, filing in the same direction, all headed toward the school they could not yet see. Across a short bridge, over the railroad crossing, and they were at the school gates.

Some students headed into the main building, chatting with classmates, while others stopped to greet friends from clubs or sports teams. A few passed by alone, eyes on the phone in their hands.

The same morning sights he witnessed every school day. The world was as it should be. Everything going swimmingly. The most important thing on everyone's minds was the exams next week.

It seemed unlikely anyone else had their first love shacked up in their apartment. Even if they did, there was no way they also had their current partner staying there, too.

"Normal is so nice."

"What are you talking about?" Mai asked, glaring at him.

"Nothing important."

"Hmph. Oh, right, Sakuta…"

"What?"

"Meet me in the empty class on the third floor for lunch."

"You going to tutor me in secret?"

"I'm just going to help you study like a normal person," she said. Then she smirked at him. "Exams are almost here."

"Well, normal *is* nice," he said.

Mai pointedly ignored this remark.

On the weekend, they moved their study sessions to Sakuta's house. Or at least, he studied while she watched.

Nodoka joined them, too, grumbling the whole time but helping him whenever he was stuck. Though she looked like she partied more than she studied, she was really good at explaining things, which he found fascinating.

Shouko was the biggest surprise. She came in while Mai and Nodoka were taking a break, and she looked over his math and science.

"You're actually good at this, Shouko?"

Little Shouko could never have solved these problems. She was still in her first year of junior high. But they were clearly easy for big Shouko.

"Well, I'm supposedly a college student."

"Wish I was, too."

With a veritable smorgasbord of ladies tutoring him to ensure he was thoroughly prepped, when exams began on Monday, December 8, he wound up furiously trying to complete his answer sheets. When you don't know the answers, tests are over in no time. But when you understand what you're doing, you feel compelled to be thorough and solve everything, which takes a ton of time. He didn't even get a chance to take a nap between tests and felt very sleep deprived.

He was so busy it felt like the week flew by.

The final exam was physics. He could tell many students had already thrown in the towel. Just as Sakuta filled in the last answer, the bell rang, and finals were over.

"Finally..."

This much thinking tires out the brain. And if your brain gets tired, it's hard to summon the energy to do anything.

As Sakuta collapsed listlessly on his desk, the rest of Class 2-1 erupted. "It's over!" "Let's do something *fun*!" "I'm so doomed..." "Let's hit the beach!" "When it's this cold out?!"

They were so wound up that they didn't even settle down during the final homeroom. Their teacher had either decided they'd earned the right to be unruly for once or had already tried to calm them down and failed, but in any case, he didn't bother raising his voice.

"Don't get so worked up that you hurt yourselves during the break."

Homeroom ended early, with the usual warning to stay safe over winter vacation.

The volume in the room got even louder. Some classes had wrapped up homeroom already and were spilling out into the halls.

The students were in post-exam party mode. Sakuta would have loved to go on a date with Mai, but she had a fashion magazine shoot that afternoon. She had to leave the moment school ended and head to a studio downtown.

Exams were over, so he didn't need to lug all his textbooks home. He shoved them into his desk, snapped his empty bag shut, and glanced around the bustling classroom.

Freed from the bondage known as studying, everyone seemed much more relaxed. It was always like this after finals ended. Another normal life thing that came around and around, and it felt singularly merciless to him right now.

"......"

His thoughts were on a junior high school girl. Little Shouko.

She was still in the hospital. Sakuta was still commuting to see her every day, even during exams—although he certainly hadn't been staying long. And each passing day proved that the anxiety he'd felt was not at all unfounded.

Her condition *was* worse than she let on.

Shouko and her room had changed dramatically over the last week. She had an IV hooked up and sometimes even needed oxygen. There were a number of medical devices lined up by her bed that he'd never seen before.

Her face and limbs were getting puffy, and each time he found her looking different, he had to rack his brain to figure out the right response. But he'd never landed on one and was simply avoiding the issue. Ultimately, all he could do was talk to Shouko like there was nothing wrong.

"Oh, there you are, Sakuta."

A familiar voice snapped him out of his reverie. One of his few friends, Yuuma Kunimi, had stepped into the room and was headed toward his seat.

"Why are you here, Kunimi?"

"'Cause I need a favor. Swap shifts with me on Sunday?"

"Date with your girlfriend?"

Yuuma was going out with a girl from Sakuta's class—Saki Kamisato, one of the classroom leaders. She was standing at the door, glancing their way. A very stylish haircut and very fashionable makeup. Even in winter, her skirt was at a very carefully managed length that prioritized style over function. And naturally, that meant bare legs. Just looking at her made him feel cold. That wasn't exclusive to Saki and was true for half the girls in the room, but…he always thought they'd be better off putting sweatpants on underneath during classes, at least. Committing to fashion was brutal.

"My team's got a surprise exhibition match."

"Oh, then fine."

"……"

He'd agreed to it, but Yuuma looked surprised.

"Should I have turned you down?"

"No, I really do need to swap that shift."

"Then what?"

"What's going on with you?"

"Huh?"

"You seem extra grumpy."

"Nah, I'm... No, you're pretty much on the money."

He'd reflexively tried to wave him off but soon realized Yuuma already knew better.

"It's just...," Sakuta said, not looking at Yuuma.

His eyes drifted around the room. A third of the students were still here, talking about after-school plans.

"I never really planned to be a high school student, but somehow I am one."

"Same here. Most of us are."

Yuuma perched on the side of Sakuta's desk.

"Makinohara?" he asked, gazing absently at the hall.

"Got it in one."

"Not exactly hard to do."

Yuuma had met little Shouko before, about a month ago. She'd come to the Minegahara culture festival, and they'd met then. He'd looked after her during the mess with the beauty contests, so they'd made quite an impression on each other.

"You're visiting her daily, yeah?"

"You and Futaba both went together a couple of days ago, right? Makinohara told me."

"I bumped into Futaba at the station on the way home, and the topic came up, so...I ended up tagging along."

He sounded a little despondent, so he must've been picturing Shouko in her hospital bed.

She'd been in good shape during the culture fest, and full of life. But now she looked like she was wasting away...

Sakuta went to see her every day, and even he was alarmed by the steady decline. The anxiety he'd felt the day he got back from Kanazawa was only growing stronger. And that feeling was making him fret. Because he couldn't do anything.

And that anxiety and fretfulness sometimes exploded even when he was nowhere near the hospital. He'd be in the middle of his daily routine and start thinking about how Shouko couldn't do these ordinary things.

Sakuta himself placed no value on the bustling classroom before him. But the reason it didn't matter to him was because he'd been born healthy. It was too ordinary, something everyone had, and so he took it for granted, never realizing how lucky he was.

"You're doing fine, Sakuta. You're doing everything you can do."

"I'm just going to see her," he said, conscious of how hoarse his voice sounded.

"Makinohara talked about you a lot," Yuuma said. "About the gifts you brought for her, how you came again the day before, Sakuta this, Sakuta that."

"......"

"If she's that obviously delighted about what you're doing, you're giving her a lot."

"A lot of what?"

"You know what I mean. So don't ask."

Yuuma hopped down off the desk.

"Hokay, I'm off to practice. Thanks for filling in for me on Sunday."

"Oh, I already forgot."

"Don't!" Yuuma said, laughing as he left.

In the hall, he started talking to Saki Kamisato. She was smiling happily. Her cheeks slightly red. Maybe Yuuma was "giving" Saki a lot, too.

"Giving, huh?"

He understood what Yuuma was getting at earlier. You can make people feel good and have fun, like they're fine the way they are, like their lives are gonna be nice and happy. Japanese people tended to avoid the word, but the rest of the world calls that *love*. Sakuta found it hard to believe he was giving anyone anything so grandiose. But another part of him wanted to be someone who could do that for those close to him.

It reminded Sakuta of the words that had meant so much to him.

The words high school Shouko had said two years ago.

——*"You see, Sakuta. I think living makes us kinder."*

He felt like this was what she'd meant.

"Wow, Shouko…how were you this wise in your second year of high school?"

Sakuta was that age himself. The same age she'd been back then. He didn't think he could even begin to do what she'd done for him. Just walking up to a strange junior high kid and talking to them was a risky proposition. They might think you were a creep. He'd literally had his butt kicked by a cute high school girl just for trying to help a lost four-year-old.

As he thought about this, his chest started to sting. He felt sweat forming. Worried, he undid a couple of buttons and peered inside his shirt.

Three scar lines. Faintly swollen with blood.

"Are these gonna heal up by Christmas?"

If what Mai had promised in Kanazawa came true, he had a really nice present waiting for him, but in his state, it was hard to relax and devote himself to flirting. He would likely be too distracted to enjoy it at all.

"I could really use a lucky break here."

"Azusagawa, what are you doing?"

He looked up from his shirt to find a girl in a white lab coat standing in front of him. Her hair was tied up, and she had a look of contempt behind her intellectual glasses.

"Some new creepy fetish?" she asked.

"Futaba, nice timing."

"I'm not helping you with that."

"It's not a fetish."

"Doesn't matter. Here."

Her expression not shifting at all, she held out her phone.

"Huh?"

He blinked at her, confused.

"Answer, and you'll see."

"Answer what?"

"The phone."

The display showed she was already connected, and he recognized the number. After all, it was the one for his apartment phone. Someone calling from his house.

"Hello?" he said, picking up.

"Oh, Sakuta!"

"Yes, this is Sakuta."

"And who am I?"

"I would hope you're the only person who'd be this obnoxious, Shouko."

"You're still at school, then. Glad she caught you. Thank Futaba for me, will you?"

"So what is it?"

Why was there a need to catch him before he left? Enough to rope Rio into it?

"I need you to go on a date with me today."

"Absolutely not."

"You that scared of Mai?"

That sounded like a challenge.

"Of course!"

Sakuta did not rise to it.

"You really don't want to upset her ever, huh?"

"Exactly."

Denying it didn't seem like it would get him anywhere, so he emphatically agreed.

"But I think this date will be to her benefit," Shouko said. There was a very deliberate purr in her voice. She was definitely leading him on.

"If I go on a date with you, will the Adolescence Syndrome resolve itself? Will you finally pass on?"

"I will."

He'd meant it as a joke and gotten a serious reply.

"I'll be pissed if you're lying."

"Stick around school for now," Shouko said, ignoring his threat. "Let's meet in front of the Hawaiian Café by the Shichirigahama parking lot."

"The Hawaiian Café?"

That was not a name he was familiar with. He had no clue what shop she was talking about.

"The fast-food place that's closing down is gonna be a Hawaiian Café in the spring, so she probably means that," Rio said.

Either Shouko was talking loudly or the phone's volume was just high enough to hear; Rio seemed to be following the entire conversation.

"Oh, there? Got it."

"Later, alligator!"

With a merry laugh, she hung up.

Sakuta pressed the end call button and handed the phone back to Rio. She took it, then gave him a meaningful glare.

"I'll tell Mai myself, so you don't need to."

"I didn't say a word."

"But you looked at me like I was pond scum."

"That's how I always look at you."

"That's cruel in its own way."

But Rio was still glaring at him.

"Have something else to say?"

"Nothing major."

"Well, spit it out already."

"Nah, never mind."

"Okay, now I'm really curious. At this rate, I won't sleep a wink tonight."

"If I say it, you'll be sleepless for days."

She did not seem to be joking. There was a grim gleam in her eyes. Which forced Sakuta's hand.

"Then I *really* need to know."

Rio let out a short sigh. Then she looked him in the eye again.

"Azusagawa, what are your feelings for Shouko?" she asked.

"Well...she's my first love."

That fact didn't change, whether he was dating Mai or not.

"I don't mean that."

"Mm?"

What was she driving at?

"Let me rephrase...Who exactly *is* Shouko?"

"Shouko Makinohara."

Nothing more, nothing less.

"When I was two people, both of us were clearly Rio Futaba, enough that I knew the other one was also 'Rio Futaba.'"

"Uh, right."

Sakuta himself had been unable to declare one of them a fake. He remembered thinking they both seemed like the real deal. It had been a very strange feeling.

But in this case, the girl he called "Makinohara" and the girl he called "Shouko" left very different impressions, so much so it was hard to see them as the same person.

He was beginning to get a glimmer of Rio's point. She had to be talking about that unsettling discrepancy between the two.

"If we assume the older Shouko is little Shouko's dream of the future, then how does the older Shouko perceive her own existence?"

She was talking to Sakuta but most likely wasn't expecting an answer. The thought she was voicing was half-formed, and that was why it came out as a question.

"Your personality is defined by the time you've lived and the experiences you've had. In other words, who you are is determined by your accumulated memories."

"Yeah..."

That concept was a little too familiar. Memories and personalities. Kaede's dissociative disorder had taught him just how closely linked those two were. When Kaede had lost her memories, a new Kaede was born. And when the old Kaede's memories returned, the other Kaede's personality disappeared. That was all not long ago, and his feelings about it were still pretty raw.

"By that logic, what memories are creating Shouko? If we take her word for it, she's nineteen. That's six or seven years the little one doesn't have."

"You think it can't be *only* Makinohara's dreams of her future self?"

"What would fill in all the memories of those extra years?"

That was a tough question. But it was enough to make him understand Rio's concern. Especially since she'd *just* said that your personality was defined by your memories.

"Blank spaces and fragments wouldn't be nearly enough," he concluded.

"Even if there were some blanks, that would also reflect in her personality."

It certainly had with the two Kaedes. Both had been upset by the missing memories. But Shouko showed no signs of hesitation or uncertainty. Her words came easily and clearly, and the wisdom of her added years had been real enough to save Sakuta. Twice.

And the words that had resonated the most…

——*"I've lived this long so that I could become as kind as I am now."*

What experiences could have led her to that concept?

——*"Each day, I try to be just a little nicer than I was the day before."*

How did one acquire the kindness to soothe a wounded soul?

"Do you have a working hypothesis that can explain this?"

"……"

"You must have something."

Rio wouldn't bring it up if she didn't.

"It's a ridiculous fantasy," she whispered. "But I did think of one possibility."

"And that is?"

"But if it's true, then Shouko's hiding a bombshell from us."

Her piercing gaze shot right through him.

"I think a good man laughs when a girl fools him."

That elicited a smile that didn't reach her eyes, but it soon faded. And she began to describe her "fantasy."

"She's..."

4

After a long talk, Rio said she was going to Science Club, so they split up at the shoe lockers. He thought she should at least take the afternoon off on the final day of exams, but Rio buried herself in club tasks on a daily basis despite being the sole member.

Sakuta changed into his shoes and headed out the school gates. There were still a number of students milling around the place, and a few were leaving with him.

That lasted as far as the railroad crossing.

The warning bells rang out, and the others went, "Crap, train's coming!" and most of them broke into a run, heading for the station, which was across the bridge leading to the right. He couldn't see the station name from here, but past the bridge he could just make out the green sign hanging from Shichirigahama Station.

Sakuta alone kept going down the gentle slope toward the ocean. A gust of wind came up from the water, carrying the scent of the sea with it. At Route 134, he got stuck at a light, and when it changed, he headed for the designated parking lot.

It was a huge lot overlooking the water. He headed farther in. During the marine leisure season, it got so crowded that lines formed, but in December, there were only a few cars in it. It felt deserted.

No sign of Shouko. She must not have arrived yet.

There was a white building near the center of the lot. A month ago, it had been a fast-food place. But it had tragically shut down recently, perhaps a casualty of the recession. Such a shame—eating there while gazing at the water had been a real treat.

There were lots of cafés and restaurants around, all selling themselves on their ocean views, but this had been the only one cheap enough for a high school kid to frequent. Everywhere else was all fancy and not somewhere you could just casually pop in.

There were two flyers posted on the closed doors to the fast-food shop. One was announcing the closure, and the other was about the Hawaiian Café that would open here in the spring. Apparently, it was a branch of a local shop known for pancakes and scrambled eggs. The sort of fancy place Sakuta would never willingly go.

"You got here first, Sakuta!"

He turned at the voice and found Shouko behind him. She was in a loose-knit sweater and long skirt. She had a shawl over her shoulders. Calm winter colors. While Shouko might've been prone to playfulness, her fashion choices were simple and exuded a mature confidence.

"Did I keep you long?"

"Only, like, three minutes."

"That's enough for some instant ramen!"

With that meaningless joke, Shouko looked up at the fast-food building. It hadn't closed that long ago. It was weird how fast an unused building started to look old.

"It's not open yet, huh? I figured we could grab lunch here."

Shouko's stomach growled. It seemed she'd come prepared.

"What's Kaede up to today?" he asked, pretending he hadn't heard.

"Obviously ignoring it is actually just as bad," Shouko said, blushing slightly.

"That was quite the rumble."

"You shouldn't make jokes like that with girls."

Then what *was* the right tactic?

"Kaede said she was going to spend the day reading every book she has on her list. I did ask if she wanted to join us, but she turned me down."

"She's always been like that when she has her eyes on a book, so pay it no heed."

She had once passionately explained the importance of reading them in one sitting. That was one reason she'd had trouble keeping up with texts and messages from friends.

"And I did make lunch for her, so don't worry about that."

"I'm not, so let's get this date started."

"You just can't wait a second longer, huh?"

"I want to get this Adolescence Syndrome resolved. If that's actually possible."

He wasn't really expecting much. Nor was he about to hide that.

"Then let's go," she said, meeting his cynicism with a smile. She turned and walked away, east down Route 134. Toward Kamakura.

They walked together down the coastal road. Sakuta *did* pick the traffic side. Shouko seemed to think that was funny.

"Where we going?" he asked, before she could tease him for it.

"You'll find out when we get there!"

"Then I'll assume the worst."

She was clearly up to no good. The more delighted she seemed, the more his hackles were raised.

They were walking away from the nearest station, Shichirigahama, so Sakuta had assumed their destination was within walking distance.

But apparently he was very wrong.

Shouko walked them all the way to the next station, Inamuragasaki, and then calmly waltzed through the gates and boarded a train bound for Kamakura.

It was the same retro-styled Enoden car Sakuta rode to school every morning. Going from Fujisawa to Kamakura. The opposite of his way home.

They boarded at the head of the front car, and Shouko instantly plastered herself to the glass behind the driver, like a little kid. Sakuta stood by her side.

As the train pulled out, it showed them a view you could only see from the front car. The tracks coming toward them, the houses crowding in on either side. With the buildings this close, even at this train's sluggish speeds, it made quite an impact.

"Uh, Shouko…"

"What?"

"If we're taking the train, why walk all the way to the next station?"

It would have been much faster to get on at Shichirigahama.

"A walk by the seaside is part of the date. Take this seriously!"

For some reason, she got mad at him.

"I can handle that much walking," he said. They weren't that far apart, so it wasn't worth griping about.

"Then what?"

"Are you…up to it?"

The real Shouko—the little one—was still in the hospital. And even he could tell she wasn't doing well. When he was visiting her, he could feel a grim vibe rising up through his feet.

Despite that, the Shouko with him seemed totally healthy. Sakuta kept wondering about that and was a bit scared of the answer.

"My body is in tip-top shape. In other words, I'm *fiiiine*."

She acted like she'd just said something clever.

"Not really in a joking mood."

"I'm just trying to bring the fun!"

"Then start by making me less anxious."

"I'm seriously fine. The version of me with a serious illness and no future summoned me as a dream of her future. If I was still sick, what would be the point?"

"That's fair."

"But thanks for worrying."

"You're welcome," he said sarcastically. Eyes on the tracks in front of them.

Sakuta and Shouko took the train all the way from Inamuragasaki to the end of the line, joining the throngs at Kamakura.

There was another huge crowd on the other side of the train, waiting for it to double back. Half tourists, half locals out shopping or students on their way home.

This time their destination must've been near. Kamakura was a classic date spot.

On that assumption, Sakuta headed for the gates, but…

"We change trains here," Shouko said, pulling his arm. She led him to the transfer gates for the Yokosuka Line.

"How far are we going?" he asked, once they reached the JR platform. He didn't really expect an answer.

"You'll find out when we get there," Shouko said. Same answer. Like she'd been waiting for him to ask.

"Ugh, that's obnoxious."

They rode the Yokosuka Line for another five minutes, to the next station.

"Here we are!" Shouko announced as she hopped off the train.

One stop south of Kamakura, Zushi Station. Sakuta had never been here before. It was a little nerve-racking.

He had no way of knowing what awaited him in this unfamiliar area. It was impossible for him to guess where Shouko was leading him.

Trying to calm his nerves, he looked around but soon realized the futility of this.

Shouko had led them through the gates to a bus stop. A bus pulled in around the station roundabout, and they stepped on board.

They sat down shoulder to shoulder on a seat meant for two.

"You said 'Here we are!' a minute ago," Sakuta said, unable to let it pass without comment.

He was pretty sure if they had to take a bus, that statement had been a bit premature

"When did you become such a pedantic little nitpicker?"

"Today."

"Once again, I've changed your life."

Shouko was showing no signs of remorse. Sakuta considered a follow-up attack, but before he could, she jumped ahead of him.

"We've arrived!" she said, grinning.

The sign at the bus stop read MORITO BEACH.

He could smell the sea right away. They must've been close to the water. But he didn't recognize anything. He looked left and right, but it was all unfamiliar. A strange town and a strange road leading to places unknown.

While Sakuta's head spun, Shouko set off like she knew right where she was going. Not wanting to lose her, he followed.

"You know this area, Shouko?"

"Mm-hmm."

No reason to doubt her word. But it also sounded like she was being purposefully vague.

The roads they took were giving him déjà vu. They were a lot like the sights on the Enoden as it passed near Enoshima. The apartment buildings had a touch of resort flair to them, and lots of shops had white signs, imparting a very coastal flavor.

He found a street sign with the word HAYAMA on it. Even in the Shonan area, this was a neighborhood that had always seemed "grown-up" to him. There were probably sections of Hayama that were like that, but the one Shouko was leading him through was super ordinary.

It was just new to him. And walking down an unfamiliar street with Shouko was a strange sensation. It felt extra extraordinary.

They crossed a bridge labeled MORITO BRIDGE. Shortly after that, they turned left at a wall with a dolphin on it. Leaving the bus road and heading down a side street.

"Seriously, where are we going?" he asked. His third time asking. He didn't expect an answer. Odds were Shouko would just happily say "You'll find out when we get there!" again.

But this time he got a different reaction.

"This place," she said, stopping in her tracks. They were near a brick building. Maybe three or four stories tall. This wasn't an area filled with tall buildings, so this seemed pretty sizable.

It looked like a seaside resort hotel, with rooms and a restaurant.

That was all he got out of it; he had no idea why Shouko would bring him to a place like this.

"I am whit-free."

The clue he was searching for came from a couple who emerged from the building. They were both in their late thirties, so a grown-up couple.

"The chapel certainly earned its reputation. I say this is the place."

"So at our age, you still want to put me in a wedding dress and hold a ceremony?"

"I think your students would be delighted."

"They're the last people I want to see me like that."

"Should we make it just the two of us?"

"More trouble than it's worth. They'd just insist we hold a second ceremony for them..."

A snatch of conversation in passing.

He turned to Shouko, his eyes demanding an explanation.

"Shall we?" she asked, her smile as broad as his prospects were dim.

The form at reception read *Free Tours*, and Shouko happily wrote her name down as Shouko Azusagawa.

"Well, if I use my real name, there's a chance it'll get back to little me and stress her out."

She was making excuses before he even said anything.

When they finished the simple paperwork, a lady in a suit came out to greet them. She was in her late twenties.

"Thank you for joining us for a tour! My name is Ichihara, and I'll be your guide today. A pleasure to meet you both."

A very polite, mature greeting. Very professional.

"Are you two...?"

But then she looked at the two of them, somewhat at a loss for words.

They were both clearly a bit young to be touring wedding venues.

Sakuta had come here straight from school and was still in uniform, so Ichihara's confusion was only natural.

"I'm standing in for my sister's boyfriend. Something came up at work," he explained.

"That's right! I didn't want to come alone, and it seemed like a waste to cancel the appointment."

Shouko played along without their needing to compare notes.

"Ah, I see now. You both look so young I was feeling a bit jealo— Ahem, never mind me. Please come this way."

Ichihara clasped her file to her chest and headed down the hall.

As they followed, Shouko whispered, "You're such a liar!"

"So are you."

They exchanged glances. It hadn't been much of a con, but pulling off anything like that was a bit of a thrill.

Their first stop was the ground-floor restaurant. Ichihara explained that they could reserve the place for the after-party. The hotel had provided a few samples of the food that could be served, so they tried them. It seemed a shocking amount of food to offer with a free tour. Neither of them had eaten lunch yet, but it was more than enough to silence their growling bellies.

On the second floor, there was a large hall. This was used for receptions. Ichihara politely explained how many people the hall could hold.

Then they headed for the third floor—the top floor.

They were led to a set of double doors.

"This is the final stop on the tour," Ichihara said, building the anticipation. "If you please?" she said to no one in particular.

On her cue, the doors opened on their own.

"Wow," Shouko gasped. Evidently overcome with emotion.

Sakuta himself was struck speechless.

The chapel before them was all blue and white. The main aisle was made of glass, which reflected the sunlight pouring through the transparent ceiling and made it look like they were walking on a carpet of water.

At the end of the aisle was a huge single-pane window, and beyond that lay the visually stunning expanse of the ocean. For a moment, it seemed like the entire chapel was floating on the water.

"Go on in," Ichihara said.

Shouko headed down the virgin road. Her steps were unsteady, like a little girl lost in the world of dreams.

Sakuta elected not to say anything. He didn't want to ruin the moment, and he had to admit it did feel like he'd stepped into a dream himself. The chapel was just that unreal.

He knew now why the couple at the hotel entrance had sounded so impressed. Anyone who saw this place would want to get married here.

And Sakuta realized that what Shouko had said when she'd asked him on this date might have been true after all. The entries on the Future Schedule little Shouko had never written described them living together and then getting married. Actually getting married was out of the question, but if they came here, they could at least *feel* like they had.

"Would you like to try on a dress?" Ichihara asked after a while.

They turned back and saw a staff member standing on either side of the doors. This was why the doors had appeared to open on their own. A simple trick once you knew the truth.

"Dress…?" Sakuta asked when Shouko said nothing.

But given where they were, there was only one kind she could mean.

"A wedding dress."

"Figured."

"A few of the many gowns we offer are available to try on during the tour."

Ichihara opened the file she carried, showing them the contents. It had sample photos of a number of different wedding dresses.

"A dress? Can I?" Shouko whispered. She sounded less enthusiastic than he'd expected. Sakuta had assumed she'd leap at the chance, so this caught him by surprise. Usually, she'd be teasing him, insisting he pick a gown for her.

"Go on, try one," he said.

"But…" She hesitated, blushing slightly. Why get embarrassed when they'd already come this far?

"I think this one would look good on you," Ichihara suggested, pointing at one of the photos. A pure-white dress. Both shoulders were bare, but the overall vibe was chaste and classy.

"Still…" Shouko wavered.

Sakuta gave her a push. "Hook my sister up," he said, grinning at Ichihara.

"Will do. This way."

Shouko turned once, glaring at him, but then she followed Ichihara out. "So pushy!" she grumbled, but he pretended not to hear.

"Please wait here a bit for your sister," Ichihara requested.

"Gotcha."

Alone in the chapel, Sakuta took a seat on the front pew, wondering how long "a bit" would be.

He would usually assume it meant, like, five or ten minutes. But twenty minutes passed without any sign of Shouko returning, or Ichihara.

"Japanese is hard," he concluded.

But if he thought about it, choosing a wedding dress and putting it on would take way longer than five or ten minutes. Even by a conservative estimate, "a bit" meant, like, half an hour in a place like this.

"Hopefully, it takes only that long…"

At an actual wedding, there'd be a ton more time spent on hair and makeup. He just had to hope he wouldn't be stuck here for a full hour.

As he looped through this line of thinking, Ichihara's voice came from behind him.

"Thanks for your patience."

They'd kept him waiting for more than thirty minutes, and Sakuta turned around to complain...but the words never made it out of his mouth.

Instead, his jaw dropped.

His eyes were locked on a pure-white bride. Shouko, at the end of the aisle, in a wedding dress.

"......"

Careful not to trip over the hem of it, she came down the aisle toward him.

She was holding a small bouquet in her hands. Weddings on TV often had the brides wearing veils, but not Shouko. He could clearly see the embarrassment on her face. They had put some makeup on her, a little blush on her cheeks. Her hair had also been braided, leaving her neck and shoulders exposed to the air.

The bare skin definitely had an effect on him.

The soft fabric of the dress was draped loosely around her torso but was pulled tight at the waist. Below that, the skirts billowed out like a flower in bloom. It had the layered volume of a rose's petals. Pure and dazzling.

Sakuta stood waiting for her at the end of the aisle, in the groom's position.

"......"

He still couldn't manage speech.

Shouko reached him without either of them speaking a word.

And they stood together where couples pledged vows of eternal love.

"Your jaw's hanging open," Shouko pointed out with a giggle.

He went ahead and closed it.

"You can't tell me what you think with your mouth closed," she said, a triumphant smile playing around her lips.

"Well, you did take over half an hour, so it oughtta be at least this good."

He managed a little snark but couldn't look her in the eye as he did. The mood was a bit much. And the dress's effect—positively devastating. The makeup was really enhancing her every expression.

"Meaning?"

"You're alarmingly beautiful."

"Then it was worth the effort to pick something that would impress you."

Shouko grinned, then pulled his arm. Turning him so the sea was behind them.

"Shouko, watch your feet," he said.

One false step, and she'd trip over her own skirts.

"Come on, eyes up."

As he followed her gaze, looking down the aisle, she hugged his arm to her. Something soft pressed against him.

Sakuta reflexively glanced down. Shouko's breasts were pressed up against his arm. And something he saw there made him tense up.

"Come on, Sakuta. Get your mind out of the gutter and look up."

When he did, he saw Ichihara holding a Polaroid camera.

"Turns out, they offer a keepsake photo service," Shouko said gleefully. Her arms tightened around his. She'd dithered like hell about changing, but once she got the dress on, she was back to her usual playfulness.

"Ready? Say cheese!"

The shutter clicked.

Ichihara came over to them, fanning the photo. It was already visible by the time she handed it to them.

"Sakuta, your eyes are so dead."

Meanwhile, Shouko was positively beaming. As bright as the dress was subdued. The trace of baby face lingering in her smile only accentuated her look of joy. It was like she was so happy she was incapable of any other expression.

But Sakuta's mind was stuck on something else, and her grin wasn't infecting him. The glimpse he'd caught of her chest and what he'd seen there…

"You still have some time, so let me know when you're done. I'll be just outside."

Ichihara bowed once and left the chapel.

Sakuta and Shouko were alone together.

"……"

"……"

Neither spoke at first.

To fill the silence, he turned toward the ocean. Shouko followed suit.

If they'd had a priest present, they'd be ready to say their vows.

"The free tour gonna be enough?"

"You'd have to ask the little me that."

"I think you know without us asking."

"……"

Shouko focused her gaze on the ocean outside the chapel.

"I mean, the scar on your chest…"

He didn't mince his words at all. Couldn't think of any other way to put it. He'd spotted the scar when Shouko pulled him close for the photo. Just a glimpse of pale skin inside the dress, a single faint scar running down between her breasts. Wasn't hard to infer where it had come from. It was clear as day. There was no reason to hesitate.

"You've had a transplant."

"Mm."

Her tone didn't change. She wasn't rattled, surprised, or upset. She was so calm it was like she'd known he would bring this up.

Alone with her in the chapel, Sakuta said something he still couldn't believe yet was weirdly certain of.

"So it's true. You're from the future."

Shouko's brows twitched once, troubled, but then she let out a long sigh. Then she smiled, as if admitting he was completely right.

shouko makinohara

1

This was all part of what he'd heard earlier that day.

After big Shouko invited him on a date, Rio had told Sakuta a theory about little Shouko's Adolescence Syndrome that even she found hard to believe.

This happened three hours ago…

…in the classroom right after exams.

"She may have come from the future," Rio Futaba said, looking dead serious.

This was far too sudden for him.

"Huh?" was all he could manage.

It didn't even qualify as surprise. Unable to process what she'd said, he was just making a noise.

"Technically speaking, it may be more like she's an aspect of herself that was able to reach that future."

Even this phrasing didn't really make sense to him. He hadn't even digested the core premise yet.

Rio had said…*the future.* Before he could do anything else, he had to get a definition of that word. At the very least, it was clear Rio wasn't using *future* the way anyone else would.

"Is that the same future I know about? Like, the one that happens next year or the year after?"

He was hoping she'd say no. Otherwise they were getting into some time travel crap here. Whether she sensed his apprehension or not, Rio just nodded impassively.

"That's the one," she said.

"Oh," he said, like he understood. But if he was getting tripped up before they'd even started, there was no way he was going to make it to her actual conclusion. "Uh, how so?"

A group of lingering girls moved to the hall, laughing. Everyone else had already left, so classroom 2-1 was deserted. Just Sakuta and Rio…

"You said before that traveling into the past was problematic."

"I'm surprised you remember."

That lecture had arrived when he'd gotten swept up in Tomoe Koga's Adolescence Syndrome. Sakuta found himself repeating the same day, and Rio had told him about Laplace's demon.

"That's why I corrected myself. She didn't come from the future—she's gone there."

"So…like the petite devil, she's a future simulation?"

"That involved accurately predicting future events in full knowledge of the position and velocity of all matter in the universe, so it doesn't apply here. That wouldn't explain why we can perceive both Shoukos."

"Then…"

"Are you familiar with the Urashima Effect?"

"I know the story of 'Urashima Taro.'"

"If you hadn't known that, I'd have stopped attempting to explain *anything.*"

"Is it possible to be born in this country, reach our age, and not know that story?"

If it was, he'd like to meet a person like that. And find out what kind of messed-up life they'd led.

"So what's the gist of that story?"

"He rescues a turtle and gets taken to the Dragon Palace and, after a few days there, comes back to the surface to find decades have passed; then he opens the jeweled box and becomes an old man."

"So the key part is that a few days in the Dragon Palace are decades on the surface. In physics terms, there's a theory explaining this phenomenon."

"Who thought *that* up?"

"Einstein."

"How did he end up reading 'Urashima Taro'?"

Geniuses sure saw the world in a different light.

"'Urashima Taro' wasn't the inspiration for it or anything. Even you've heard of the theory of special relativity, right? It's on the third-year syllabus."

"Er, it is? Seriously?"

That was an alarming discovery.

"Not the whole thing, but part of it is in the textbook."

"I don't wanna be a third-year..."

"Getting held back a year at a public school spells certain doom."

"I didn't mean it that way..."

He was thinking more in Neverland terms. But regardless of his desires, Rio moved on.

"So in special relativity, the faster matter travels, the slower time flows."

"...That doesn't make a whit of sense."

"It's the result of an experiment using two extremely accurate atomic clocks..."

Rio took two pieces of hard candy out of her pocket, one blue, one red. Probably cream soda and apricot flavored.

"They put one at the starting location."

She set the blue candy on his desk.

"And the other on a plane that flew around the earth."

She waved the red candy in a circle around the desk, completing its journey back at the blue candy's position. These candies represented "extremely accurate atomic clocks," apparently.

"And what do you think happened?"

"Well, if what you just said is true, the plane is faster, so time flowed slower?" he said, pointing at the red candy.

"Yes. Fifty-nine nanoseconds slower."

"How many seconds is that?"

"One nanosecond is a billionth of second, so 59/1,000,000,000."

"Seems well within the margin of error..."

Certainly not a time difference perceivable by humans.

"That's why they used 'extremely accurate' clocks. But the fifty-nine-nanosecond discrepancy matched the mathematical solution Einstein had discovered."

"What do you have to eat to start thinking like that?"

Sakuta had been on planes and the Shinkansen and had never once stopped to consider if the flow of time was altered. He'd gone his whole life without ever entertaining such notions.

"I wouldn't know. But this proves that time is relative, not absolute."

"I don't get it. Let's just call a second a second before I get a headache."

"Azusagawa, what defines that second?"

"Well, the earth's rotation takes twenty-four hours, so you divide one of those hours by sixty to get a minute, and one of those minutes by sixty to get a second."

"That explanation is a century out of date."

"Huh?"

"Currently, a second is the duration of 9,192,631,770 periods of the radiation corresponding to the transition between the two hyperfine levels of the ground state of the cesium-133 atom."

"Come again?"

"A second is the duration of 9,192,631,770 periods of the radiation corresponding to the transition between the two hyperfine levels of the ground state of the cesium-133 atom."

Hearing it a second time did not help it enter his head. It was easier remembering the codes that allowed you to revive yourself in old video games.

"...Let's get back on track. So Shouko came from the future...or went there? How does that work?"

Rio put the candies back in her pocket. Then she looked out the window. At the waters off Shichirigahama Beach. It was a clear day, and the sunlight made the ocean glimmer.

"If someone told you you'd never survive high school, what would you do?" she asked, suddenly abandoning the topic of physics entirely.

"Uh…not sure I can answer that without it actually happening."

She was obviously asking about Shouko's state of mind. And that was exactly why he didn't want to give an easy answer. He wasn't being evasive, either; he genuinely thought it was the sort of thing you only discovered when it really happened to you.

"What do you imagine you'd do, then?"

Rio seemed hell-bent on prying an answer out of him.

"Makinohara said she wanted her parents to see her all grown up."

He remembered her sitting there on the hospital bed, her smile unfettered.

"Right."

"I wouldn't think like that. I'd be too full of my own problems to want to grow up. I'd rather stay a kid. Stay a high school student. I'd rather time just stopped for me."

"I bet Shouko feels like that, too."

"How can you be sure?"

"You weren't with us when I went to see her the other day. I think that's why she let herself grumble. She said, 'I hope my body stops growing.'"

"……"

"Maybe those feelings are why she couldn't finish the Future Schedule."

"…Makes sense."

This is simply a truth of life. It's impossible to stay positive all the time. To cling to hope. Sometimes anxiety and worries will weigh you down. Shouko was no exception. No way was she going through life with her eyes fixed permanently on a hopeful future.

She'd have nights alone in the hospital, wondering what would happen if they never found a donor. If her body gave out before then. It would be scary. She would hope she never grew up. She would wish that tomorrow wouldn't come. These thoughts were only too natural.

"One side of Shouko hopes she grows up, and another hopes she never does. And the latter one…I think that fear is what created the older Shouko."

"Hmm? Wouldn't the hopeful side be more likely?"

"If you really have faith in the future, there's no need to rush to it."

"Fair enough."

She'd really hit the target dead center.

"Which brings us back to the topic of time."

"And how it's relative?"

"The side of Shouko that doesn't want to grow up is desperately trying to stop her internal clock. She's averting her eyes from the future, hunkering down, trying to make herself stop."

"…A complete standstill."

"And what if the result is that the world she sees *is* getting slower, like everything is in slow motion? And seen from the world where we are, where the Shouko who wants to grow up is, what happens in relative terms?"

"Okay, stop, Futaba."

He understood her conclusion, at least. Time flowed slower when moving faster—she'd just explained this. But before they could even get to that, there was a major question occupying his mind.

"You're saying there are two worlds?"

"That was my intention, yes."

"You make it sound simple."

He almost managed a chuckle.

"I figured you'd figure it out without the steps in between."

"You clearly think too highly of me."

"Fine…"

Rio took two candies out of her pocket again and placed them on the desk. This time they were purple and green. Presumably grape and muscat flavored.

"Let's say the purple one is the Shouko who wants to grow up and the world we see that moves at normal speeds. But the green one is the Shouko who doesn't want to grow up and is in slow motion."

"Is it just normal for there to be multiple worlds?"

"A matter of perspective, but potentially infinite."

"Are you serious?"

"There's no guarantee the world you see and the world I see are the same. If we discuss it in micro terms, you remember me telling you about how the location of particles only goes from a probability to a fixed point through the act of observation?"

"Oh, quantum physics. My favorite."

The idea that something could exist in a state of probability only until it was observed just sounded like magic. But it was apparently the truth. Thinking about that principle in terms of his own body made him afraid he was fading away. Although that obviously wasn't the case.

"If the discrepancy between the speeds of the purple and green worlds is sufficient, then what does the slower green world look like viewed from the faster purple world?"

If he'd followed Rio's lecture this far, the answer was simple.

"Like time's moving faster in the green world."

"Yes. In other words, the faster time flows for Shouko who rejects growing up—basically the older Shouko—the further ahead of us in time she gets."

"It's starting to add up."

He finally grasped what Rio meant.

"Talk about irony."

She was trying so hard not to grow up that she'd somehow wound up in the future… You couldn't get much more ironic.

"Yeah."

"So why is the grown-up Shouko from the green world here in the purple one?"

"By way of explanation, I placed the two worlds next to each other, but a probabilistic interpretation suggests the worlds are overlapping."

"Overlapping?"

"Does it make sense if I say it's right next to us, we just can't see it?"

"...Kinda, kinda not."

He looked at the empty chair next to him. Rio was saying another world existed, just one he couldn't see, touch, or perceive.

"Normally, we can only perceive one of these two worlds, but whether by chance or fate, we've realized the other Shouko exists. That's our current situation."

This, too, he sorta got but sorta didn't. But Sakuta didn't really see the point in mastering the underlying principle. What he needed to know was what came after that.

"So my other question..."

"What?"

"If Shouko has reached the future, wouldn't that eliminate the anxiety causing the Adolescence Syndrome? I mean, she knows she'll be a high school student. And a college student."

If the source of her anxiety was gone, that should resolve the Adolescence Syndrome. And that would also mean there was no reason for big Shouko to be here.

"I'm not so sure. Anxiety isn't a one-off deal, and if it really is little Shouko's Adolescence Syndrome, and if she doesn't know about big Shouko, then you could argue she has no way of knowing that big Shouko made it to the future."

"Good point. But in that case, wouldn't telling her fix things?"

A secure future. That was what little Shouko most wanted. A ticket to a future that could wash away her fears.

"Potentially."

But there was something they had to verify before they could hand over that ticket.

"How do you propose we prove this hypothesis?"

At present, this was all pure conjecture on Rio's part. They had no solid evidence to speak of.

If there was any evidence that proved this theory beyond a doubt, the only one aware of them was big Shouko. But for whatever reason, she had yet to breathe a word of any of this. Even if they asked her point-blank what she was hiding, it seemed unlikely she would just tell them.

If she was keeping something this important from them, there must've been a reason for it.

"Azusagawa, find an excuse to look down her shirt."

"Hngg?"

This strange noise was a direct result of Rio's abrupt swerve. Of all the proposals she could have made, she went there?

"If Shouko really is the future of little Shouko, then that's where you'll find proof."

Looking dead serious, Rio drew a line down her chest, right between her boobs.

"The transplant scar."

"......"

The only way Shouko could have a chance to grow up. A heart transplant. Without that, she'd never live to see high school, much less college. If she'd survived, she must have had the surgery.

"The Future Schedule homework never mentioned the surgery, and it never came up when little Shouko talked about what she wanted to add...so if the scar is there, that should clinch it. The older Shouko isn't a dream little Shouko is having, but her actual future."

"But even if that logic holds true, you should really be the one looking."

"Why?"

"You're a girl."

"But you're way more interested in staring at girls' cleavage."

"It's a matter of difficulty."

Things other girls were allowed to do could well become criminal acts when men did them.

"And I think this is something you're better off seeing with your own eyes, Azusagawa."

"……"

"You're definitely one of those people who has to see it to believe it."

Rio was being all grim and acting like the discussion was already over. It wasn't the most concrete argument he'd ever heard, but he had to admit it rang true. Rio knew Sakuta pretty well. But he wished she also knew that he believed basically anything she said without needing to confirm it first.

"Okay, fine. So practically speaking, just what excuse will convince a girl to let you look at her boobs?"

"Maybe after a bath?"

"She comes out in pajamas."

Shouko's outfits were all pretty conservative. He'd never even seen her in short sleeves.

Maybe she was deliberately avoiding showing skin. That might be overthinking it, but…

"Then maybe hide a spy cam in your bathroom?"

Was it his imagination, or was she already giving him a look of contempt?

"If I actually did that, what would you do?"

"Call the cops."

"Then why suggest it?"

"Another option is to just take a run at Shouko, seduce her, and get her clothes off. I mean, you love her, right?"

This conversation was getting out of hand. If the look in her eyes was anything to go by, she was clearly testing him.

If he broke eye contact here, he was sunk.

And if he lied, she'd nail him with something worse.

So Sakuta decided to own it.

"I love her," he said.

"As a person?" Rio sneered.

He would really prefer it if she didn't close off his escape routes like that, but he wasn't about to let her render him speechless, either.

"As a woman," he said, electing to take the bait.

His first love may not have borne fruit, but that didn't sour his feelings for Shouko. When he'd made it to Minegahara and found no signs of her, there was no outlet for his feelings, and over time, they'd simmered down. That was all. They hadn't gone anywhere, and they hadn't magically ceased to exist. With Shouko back at arm's length, his old feelings *had* come boiling back up. And he didn't hesitate to give them a proper name.

"That's very *you*, Azusagawa. I can see why Sakurajima's worried."

"I'm sure Mai reads me like a book."

If he dismissed his feelings for Shouko, Mai would hate him for it. She knew just how much Shouko had been there for Sakuta, and any signs that he failed to comprehend that would only earn Mai's contempt.

But that didn't mean she was prepared to accept it from an emotional perspective.

Undoubtedly, she was conflicted. But that was what happened when emotions and logic were saying contradictory things. Sakuta didn't think either side was absolutely right. His only real option was to try to find a middle ground, not leaning too far to either side. Sometimes the balanced path was the right choice.

"Also, perhaps this is beside the point, but..."

"Mm?"

"If Shouko really is the future version of little Shouko, then that might explain why they're so different."

"I imagine getting a heart transplant would have an effect on your outlook."

The candle of her life had been about to burn out, and then the operation gave her a massive extension. The same kind of candle everyone else had, one where she had no idea how long it would burn. She'd be overjoyed yet also at a loss. It only made sense that it would uproot how she thought and felt about everything. It would be far stranger if she stayed the same.

"You see stories about it on TV sometimes, claiming that patients who got a heart transplant also receive fragments of the donor's memories or personalities. And researchers have actually found cells in human organs that can harbor memories."

"Then the way she deliberately ignores social cues comes from the donor?"

"That's one possibility. A more reasonable assumption is what you already said, that life-and-death operations do tend to change your perspective."

This new idea was just one other potential explanation. With that made clear, Rio glanced at the classroom clock. Ten minutes until he'd agreed to meet Shouko. If he was late, Lord only knows what she'd force him to do to make up for it. Better get going.

"Not to circle back around—but Shouko is likely hiding something."

"I know. If she really is from the future, then that means Makinohara will live…and we know how this Adolescence Syndrome will work out."

Yet Shouko acted like she had no idea and gave them a different explanation entirely. She'd lied about it. To their faces. Without batting an eye.

"I suppose the most positive spin you could put on it is that, like in time travel novels, she's afraid you might change the future."

"But given her personality, it might just be for kicks."

"True." Rio nodded. She obviously didn't buy that explanation, but they were out of time to argue the point.

He checked the clock again. Only seven minutes left.

So he picked up his bag and headed for the door.

He'd just have to ask Shouko herself.

2

The two of them were walking along the deserted beach together.

A trail of their footprints ran along the sandy edge of the surf.

Sakuta and Shouko had left the wedding venue and headed down to Morito Beach. Neither had suggested it, but their feet had naturally carried them toward the water.

"......"

"......"

When their conversation trailed off, the lapping waves filled the silence.

It was a gentler sound than the waves at Shichirigahama. The same sea, but a different aspect of it.

"Futaba does not disappoint," Shouko said at last. "I didn't think I'd dropped that many hints."

"One false note, and she'll start to question every assumption."

If the equation didn't solve cleanly, she'd start wondering what was wrong. Then she'd go back over her work, trying to find the error. Rio had once explained that her brain just did that without her conscious participation. That this was the only way she could feel secure.

"She's amazing."

"I know, I know."

"I'm not complimenting you, Sakuta."

"Futaba is my lifelong friend," he said, puffing out his chest.

Shouko rolled her eyes at him and snorted.

"......"

"......"

"Um, Sakuta...," she said, then hesitated. He sensed a hint of worry in her gaze. "Are you mad?"

"Not really," he said, staring straight ahead.

"But you haven't looked at me in several minutes."

"I'm just..."

He'd meant to keep his tone level, but his voice betrayed his intentions, and he broke off. There was a burning heat behind his nose, and he couldn't get the words out. The feelings welling up inside him were belatedly spilling over.

Struggling to contain them, he tried again.

"I'm just..." But his voice was a squeak, utterly failing to disguise anything. It was wet with invisible tears. "...I'm just relieved."

The heat behind his eyes was getting worse, so he stopped and turned to look at Shouko. She stopped, too, returning his gaze.

Shouko was right here, with him. Her long hair blowing in the sea breeze, held back by her pale hand. She looked slightly annoyed by the force of the wind, but there was a trace of a smile on the corners of her lips and a gentleness in her eyes. As Sakuta tried not to cry, she watched wordlessly over him.

"Makinohara's gonna get the operation she needs, right?"

Shouko was from the future. She was little Shouko's future.

"She is." Shouko nodded.

"She'll make it to high school."

"You met her two years ago."

"And college... She'll get to grow up."

"Do I look like a junior high school kid to you?"

"If a junior high school kid looked as old as you do, it would be on the news."

"You couldn't have just said I'd grown into a real beauty and left it at that?" She sulked.

"I'm just...really glad."

The tension keeping him going was suddenly gone, and his strength left him. He crouched down on the sand. Shouko's deteriorating condition had taken more of a toll on him than he'd realized. And having that fear snatched away yanked the rug out from under him.

"Sakuta?" Shouko leaned in to check on him.

"I'm just relieved," he said again.

He couldn't find the strength to stand, and that fact made him laugh.

He hadn't realized just how much the anxiety had mushroomed within him. Maybe a part of him had even started to give up hope.

Not a good sign.

The seed of doubt planted that day had grown each time he told himself it would all be fine, spreading roots deep inside, a stalk shooting up through his entire body.

"Time will solve everything."

"......"

He looked up, and Shouko's smile wrapped around him like a warm beam of sunlight.

"Little me's heart condition."

"......"

"And little me's Adolescence Syndrome."

Shouko spoke slowly, each word distinct.

"It'll all be over by Christmas."

"You mean..."

Shouko put her hands to her chest.

"Little me will have her operation soon and no longer have to worry about her heart."

"And you'll..."

"So I can only be with you until Christmas."

If she had her surgery, little Shouko's anxieties about growing up would naturally go away. And the Adolescence Syndrome caused by those emotions would be resolved. It made sense.

Shouko reached out both hands toward him. Sakuta took them, and she pulled him to his feet. Like she was proving how healthy she was.

"Sakuta."

"Yes?"

"Give me one last memory?"

"Like what?"

"The first-love kind."

She made it sound so simple and direct, he started blushing, and when she saw that, she turned red, too.

"Why are *you* the one blushing?" she asked.
"I'm just excited."
"Don't try to distract me! Answer the question."
He'd hoped to wriggle out of it, but it wasn't that easy.
"Honestly, that's the thing I don't get about you, Shouko."
"Meaning?"
She knew exactly what he meant but asked anyway.
"Even when Mai was there...," he started, but then he realized that was definitely not a subject he should broach and cut himself off.
But Shouko pounced on it. "That reminds me, Sakuta," she said.
"Of what?" He tried playing dumb. But he'd brought it up, so he couldn't get out of it now.
"I still haven't heard back."
"Heard what?"
"Your answer."
"To what?"
"My confession."
"Of your sins?"
"Of my love."
"......"
"Ugh, Sakuta, you *know* what I mean."
For all her protests, she was clearly enjoying this tug-of-war.
"I'm clueless."
"You're such a liar!"
"I dunno why you'd love me."
"......"
Shouko looked at him like he was a bizarre sea creature. She blinked several times. Like she had no clue why he wouldn't get something that obvious.
"I had any number of reasons to be drawn to you, Shouko, but..."
"Like the time I put my arms around you, pressed myself up against your back, and offered to kiss you?"
"That's enough to snare any junior high boy."

At that age, you could even fall in love with the cute girl in front of you just because she picked up the eraser you dropped.

"But there was more than that."

"You told me the distance to the horizon and the three words you loved most, and you taught me the meaning of life."

He understood now why she'd been able to do that. After years spent with death close at hand, the transplant had given her life a future. Her experience with her condition had left Shouko deeply grateful. For the parents and people around her who'd supported her, for the courage of the donor and their family in the face of whatever tragic accident or illness befell them. Shouko had so much to be grateful for, had gained so much from the kindness of others, that she'd been able to acquire such wisdom.

At the time, he hadn't even begun to understand what she meant. Maybe he'd still barely scratched the surface. But just remembering it made him want to cry. Especially knowing how it was born of all the kindness that had prolonged her life.

"So I made a man out of you, Sakuta?"

She was deliberately choosing that phrasing. Probably half to cover her own embarrassment. But the other half was just teasing Sakuta.

"I don't remember making a woman of you," he said, fighting back.

"You're the one who made it so I could look after Hayate," she said, dodging under his blow but sounding like she meant it.

"That was just..."

"And it was you who taught me to stop saying 'Sorry' and tell Mom and Dad 'Thank you' and 'I love you' instead."

"......"

"You always treated me like I was normal, like my condition didn't matter. When I was in the hospital and sure this was it, you showed up every day to see me."

"That was all I *could* do."

"I was really glad you kept coming. I'd start getting excited when it was time for your classes to let out, and I'd look for you outside the window, peer out in the hall to see if you were there yet…and check the mirror to see if my hair looked weird and practice smiling normally. I'd get depressed about how pale I looked, and I even asked Mom if there was any way I could hide it with makeup. All worked up and hopelessly in love with you."

"……"

"Little me hadn't realized it was love yet."

"Then *you* probably shouldn't be telling me about it."

He said that to try to deflect the direction this was going, but she just laughed, clearly seeing right through it, and ignored him completely.

"But little me's first love stayed with her. She never told anyone."

"Thorny."

"I'm in college now! I'll never get a boyfriend if I keep dragging my first love around like this. You've gotta help me here."

"It's your fault I dragged *my* first love out as long as I did."

He'd even picked his high school because he was chasing after her. That was plenty cringey.

"Sakuta, you found a new woman and overcame it, so you don't get to talk."

She was definitely deliberately taking a dig at him there.

"Then what kind of memory are you looking for here?"

"Take me to see the Enoshima Illumination on Christmas Eve."

Little Shouko had mentioned she wanted to see that. It was probably something that meant a lot to Shouko. To the little one, to the big one, to all versions of Shouko Makinohara.

"Christmas Eve, huh?"

There were lots of demands on him that day. Mai, of course. And he couldn't just abandon Kaede for it. But before he could bring any of that up…

"Don't worry," Shouko said, like she could see the future. "Kaede's going to stay with your grandparents on the twenty-third."

First he'd heard of it.

"She'd going to give you and your wonderful girlfriend some space."

If this prophecy was true, it would definitely prove Shouko was from the future.

"My sister knows what's up, huh?"

But what were Mai's plans? Would she just end up taking more work and being too busy to spend time with him? Maybe that was why Shouko had chosen to invite him.

"Don't worry," Shouko said again, grinning at him. "Mai will have the evening off, so you can relax."

That was certainly good news, but didn't that make the situation even messier? Or maybe not. Maybe it was really simple.

"You'll have to decide what to do, Sakuta. Spend that time with me, or spend it with Mai."

There was a trace of sadness to her smile. But Sakuta finally realized what it was she was after.

"I'll be waiting at the dragon lantern by the entrance to Benten Bridge at six PM on December twenty-fourth."

"Shouko, I..."

"You don't need to say it. But I'll be waiting there."

She was back to her usual impish smile.

And that left him with no option but to swallow his words. That was what Shouko wanted him to do. And his actions on December 24 would have to be his answer.

His father called that night. He had a lot of opinions about Sakuta's love life, but that wasn't why he'd called. Now that Kaede's dissociative disorder had cleared up, her grandparents wanted to see her again. They hadn't seen her once in two years.

So starting on the twenty-third, she'd be visiting their grandparents for a few days. Their father would be stopping by, too.

Just what Shouko had said would happen.

This definitely rattled him. And planted a growing certainty in his mind.

Kaede made a face and then said, "It's better if I'm not around for Christmas, right?"

Shouko's prediction had even been accurate down to his sister's motives.

3

The day after his surprise date with Shouko—Saturday, December 13—Sakuta was working the late shift until nine, and he hit the bath the second he got home.

The hot water soothed the fatigue of a long day. If he could get Mai to coddle and scold him, he'd be fully recovered, but when he got out of the bath, she still wasn't home.

He poked his head into the living room, still drying his hair. No Mai.

"You hear anything from Mai?" he asked. Kaede was at the *kotatsu*, watching TV. Shouko was taking her turn in the bath. He could hear the shower running. And her humming.

"Not yet."

Mai had left early for her film shoot. The same one they'd done location work for in Kanazawa. They still had some interior scenes left, and they were shooting those on a soundstage in Tokyo.

But it was pretty late. He glanced at the clock above the TV; it was ten past ten.

Kaede was channel surfing.

"Anything on?" he asked, finally done drying his hair.

"So many people I don't know. It's hard to follow anything."

A two-year gap in your memories would do that.

She stopped on a talk show. A comedy duo was performing their routine. Their bit was unfolding at a blistering pace.

"Is this what's funny now?"

"They're on TV a lot, so I guess so?"

"If people quote this at school, I'll be in trouble. I don't get it at all."

Kaede collapsed on the *kotatsu*, her face turned toward the screen.

"No need to force yourself."

"Ugh. How am I supposed to make friends?"

"You'll just have to write your own routine. 'My body's third-year, but my mind is still first-year!' Make the whole class laugh."

"That discrepancy is the problem! Why do you think I've been on a TV binge?"

Kaede glared at him, but this was not the least bit intimidating. It just looked sulky.

"Hard to cram two years' worth before third term starts."

Kaede was busy working toward returning to school. Their father had already spoken to the school, and after classes ended on Wednesday, her school counselor, Miwako Tomobe, had stopped by to see her. She'd definitely been a little rattled by how different Kaede was, but they'd talked for a while and set some goals.

And one of those was to attend school starting from third term.

"That's the problem!"

"So make a joke of it."

"And draw attention to myself?"

"You're joining the class in third term; there's no avoiding that. If you make it something everyone can laugh about, it'll be way easier in the long run."

"Who am I supposed to make laugh in the nurse's office?"

Third-year students were right in the middle of entrance exam hell by this time of year. Out of consideration for that, she was going to start by hanging out in the nurse's office and proceed from there.

"Well, the nurse."

"Fat lot of good that does me."

Scowling, she picked up a mirror from the tabletop. Examining her face from every angle. It had changed enough over the last two years that she was still struggling to accept it.

"Do I even look like a third-year?"

"Sure. You're tall enough."

She was five foot four and change. Tall for her age.

"Won't everyone else be more grown-up?"

The TV went to a commercial break. Hearing a voice they recognized, they both turned toward the screen. Mai was there, advertising cell phones. One with a family plan. Mai was playing one of a high school couple and jokingly said, "Should we make a family, then?"

Sakuta was instantly mesmerized. He almost cried "Yes!" out loud.

Kaede was gazing at Mai with rapt attention, too. Eyes sparkling with admiration. Then she started tugging at hair, frowning.

"Kaede."

"What?"

"Mai's real cute, right?"

"I still can't believe you're dating."

"Also, Kaede..."

"What?"

"Raising ducks won't make a swan."

"Obviously."

She clearly didn't catch his drift.

"I just wanna go from a lame duck to a normal duck," she said.

Maybe she understood more than he first suspected. She was still tugging her hair.

"Well, can't hurt to try a haircut," he said.

Kaede let go.

"That wasn't what I...," she spluttered.

"I know a girl who was a real hick in junior high, but she totally transformed herself into a fashion-conscious high school girl. Now she has all kinds of guys gunning for her."

This was Tomoe Koga. She'd once shown him a picture of herself in junior high, and *hick* was the only word for it. Two clunky braids just hanging there, totally uncool. But she'd changed her hair, learned how to use makeup, and put in the work required to be a cool girl. Maybe Kaede could, too.

"Haircuts are a huge move," Kaede said.

"It takes a ton of courage just to step through the doors of those fancy salons."

"First you need to get a haircut good enough that they'll even let you in a place like that."

"Where do you get that, then?"

"That's what I wanna know."

Kaede sighed dramatically. As if trying to cheer her up, their tricolored cat, Nasuno, rubbed her back against Kaede. Maybe she was just itchy. Nasuno curled up on the warm *kotatsu* blanket.

"I guess I could give you a basic cut. That's what I've been doing."

After all, the other Kaede had been unable to leave the house.

"...Is that why the left and right are different lengths?"

"So that's a no? Then we'll have to ask Mai. Maybe she can get her stylist to take a look at you."

"I—I couldn't! I'm not worthy!"

"Oh?"

"And it'd be expensive!"

"Sure, but my wages can cover it."

"It'd be, like, ten thousand yen!"

"If it gives you the confidence to go to school, it's a bargain."

"R-really?" Kaede hesitated, toying with her hair again. Both hands. Changing her hairstyle seemed like a big step for her. But by the time the commercial ended, she whispered, "Maybe I should."

It felt like she was taking a positive step forward. Sakuta detected a genuine desire to ready herself for attending school again. Her hands were clutched at her chest. Perhaps she was thinking about the other Kaede, the one who'd spent two years steadily working toward this goal. It looked like she was swearing an oath to make that work pay off and make her return to school a success.

"All right! I'll go get the scissors."

"I'm not asking *you*! It'll be all uneven again."

She put her hands up, fending him off. Why did her strenuous objections make him want to cut her hair so bad?

He considered actually fetching the scissors, but his terrible idea was interrupted by a phone ringing. The landline.

The number on the little monochrome display was eleven digits, starting with 090. He knew that number. One of three numbers he had memorized. It was neither Yuuma's nor Rio's. This was Mai.

He picked up the phone and held it to his ear.

"Azusagawa speaking."

"This is Sakurajima. Can I speak to Sakuta?"

She knew full well it was him on the phone but went the formal route anyway. Probably because he'd answered like the call was from a stranger.

"I beg your pardon. Which Sakurajima might that be?"

"The Sakurajima currently dating Sakuta."

"What's up, Mai?" he asked, not seeing another exit from this phone-manners role play.

"We just finished filming, so I'm still at the studio. I'll be back late."

"What time?"

It was already past ten. Almost ten thirty.

"I've gotta change still, so after eleven."

"Your manager gonna drop you off?"

"The trains should get me there faster, so I was going to take one back."

She sounded unsure why he'd asked that.

"Then gimme another call before you hop on the train."

"Why?"

"So I can meet you at the station."

"I'm not a child. I'll be fine."

"You not being a child is why I'm concerned."

"I think you are the single greatest threat to me."

"I've always wanted to be dangerous! I'm honored you think of me that way."

"Okay, okay. But sure. We do need to talk, so come meet me."

"Talk about what?"

"You'll find out soon enough."

"Don't get my hopes up."

"Expect great things," Mai said with a happy laugh. Since they were on the phone, it felt like she was giggling right in his ear, which was delightful. "I'll check the train schedule and call you back."

"Okay. You did good work filming today, Mai!"

"Thanks!"

They hung up, still laughing.

Mai called again twenty minutes later. She said her train was scheduled to arrive at eleven thirty.

Fifteen minutes before that, he pried himself out of the *kotatsu*.

"I gotta go," he said.

"Stay warm!" Shouko called out, glancing over her shoulder at him.

Kaede was sitting at the *kotatsu* next to her, fast asleep. He'd told her to sleep in her bed, but she'd said she had something to talk to Mai about and, until five minutes ago, had insisted she could stay up and wait. She probably wanted to talk about the haircut before her resolve wavered. She'd been discussing what look she should go for with Shouko earlier.

"Huh? Are you back already?" she asked blearily.

"Oh, did I wake you?"

"I wasn't asleep…"

She *totally* was. She was still half-asleep now. And not only was Sakuta not back, he hadn't even left yet. But he decided not to rain on her positivity.

"I'm going to get her now," he said and left the house.

Outside, the cold night air made him shiver. There was nobody on the streets, only an eerie hush.

The chill lent wings to his feet, and he made it to the station in record time.

He went through Fujisawa Station on a daily basis, but this close to Christmas, it seemed like a totally different place.

The holiday itself was over a week away, but they already had the station covered in Christmas lights and decorations.

Fighting against the stream of people heading home, Sakuta made his way to the lockers outside the JR gates and stopped there. These lockers were where Mai had been stashing her bunny-girl outfit when they first met. It was now safely in his bedroom closet. It had been a while since he'd convinced her to put it on, though.

"Maybe she'll wear it for Christmas."

"Absolutely not."

Mai had come up behind him while he was distracted by the lockers.

"Aww. But it's Christmas!"

He hung his head, turning toward her. And found her glaring at him. She had on a knit cap with ear flaps and a mask to ward off colds. It also had the notable side-benefit of making it nigh impossible for anyone to realize they were on the same train as Mai Sakurajima.

"That is not a reason."

She started walking.

"I'd settle for miniskirt Santa."

"Christmas isn't a cosplay holiday."

"No, but it is a day for couples to flirt like mad."

"Sigh..."

He headed back the way he'd come, with Mai at his side. They passed the electronics store, following the main drag.

As the bridge came into sight, Mai suddenly asked, "So what happened with Shouko?"

This was uncanny, and his heart nearly leaped out of his chest.

"What happened how?" he said, playing dumb to cover.

"That's what I'm asking." Mai glared at him. This was just a feint, though. She wasn't actually mad. Yet.

"Nothing happened," he lied. Highly conscious of her eyes on him.

He wasn't sure what had prompted that question, but it was true there had been a major development.

Big Shouko's big secret.

Sakuta now knew the truth about who she was.

The fact that she'd come from the future…

And he hadn't told Mai this. Or anyone. Only three people knew about it: Rio, who'd first suspected it, Shouko herself, and Sakuta.

And on their way home from the wedding venue, on the Enoden train back to Fujisawa Station, Shouko had been very specific about it.

"I want you to keep this our secret."

"Futaba already knows."

"I can't have the future changing on me. If something happens that prevents the transplant, I'm doomed."

Her tone had been relaxed, but it was a clear warning. He'd taken the hint and nodded. She hadn't left him with much choice. He really didn't want a future happening where little Shouko didn't survive her condition. Now that he knew she'd make it, there was no need to consider any alternatives.

Knowledge influences the way people behave. Sakuta's own actions had likely been changed already. The way he treated little Shouko would probably be different. He'd choose different words to say to her. If there was any chance of something that minor changing the future, then the fewer people who knew the truth, the better. After all, there was no way for him to go back to not knowing.

And that was why he hadn't told Mai. Not because he was afraid she'd find out they'd visited the wedding venue and he was trying to hide that. Almost certainly not that.

"If you don't want to tell me, fine."

Mai was staring straight ahead, totally striking a "Whatever" vibe. Like she was okay with this, but she wasn't sure he should be.

"There really wasn't anything. Why do you ask?"

"The two of you seemed different last night."

"......"

She had a keen eye.

Maybe he would be safer to admit to some of it, while leaving out the part about the future. In other words, quit using Shouko's request as an excuse to get out of saying anything.

"Actually, we went to see a chapel in Hayama in secret."

"......"

This silence was terrifying.

"Shouko suggested it might help with the Adolescence Syndrome, so..."

He was choosing his words carefully, monitoring her reaction.

"Sakuta."

"Yes? What?"

"I didn't want to know."

"Then why'd you ask?"

"So this is my fault?"

"No, entirely mine."

"......"

More silence. She would normally at least manage an exasperated sigh, but not today.

"You really oughtta be meaner to me," he said.

"Then let me ask a different question."

"Gladly."

"What does Shouko mean to you?"

Mai really knew how to hit him where it hurt. Merciless topic selection. Too merciless. He'd already been feeling backed into a corner, and now she was raining blows down on him.

"She's my first love."

"Is that all?"

The look in her eyes suggested she knew something. Sakuta saw his own face reflected in them and glanced away.

Meeting Shouko again had made his feelings clear.

The truth nature of the emotions he'd been referring to as his first love.

He could say it now. A simple, short phrase that communicated everything.

It had started two years ago, when he'd first met high school Shouko. Sakuta had felt hopelessly powerless, unable to save Kaede from the bullies at school. His regrets had been so strong they'd triggered his own Adolescence Syndrome, leaving him with mysterious gashes on his chest. He'd been at rock bottom. And feeling like there was no way to pull himself back up.

But then a high school girl saved him.

Shouko saved him.

A girl he just happened to meet on the beach at Shichirigahama.

Her words had resonated with him. She'd forgiven his weakness, his inability to do anything. She'd listened to his regrets. She'd taught him the meaning of kindness. And she'd given him the strength to look up again.

All of that was what he wanted to do for Kaede. What he had failed to do.

That was why he looked up to her.

Why he wanted to be like Shouko.

His feelings for her were pure and powerful.

And at that age, he'd never had feelings like that for anyone. They were so strong that, at the time, he'd mistaken them for love.

That was Sakuta's first love.

Perhaps the right answer to Mai's question was that he admired Shouko, that she was his hero.

But even if that was the true nature of his feelings, he didn't think it was the right answer to Mai's question. It *had* been Sakuta's first love, mistakes and all. He was fine with that. First loves were often composed of feelings you didn't really understand. That was how they should be.

So no matter how many times Mai asked, his answer wouldn't change.

"Shouko's the first girl I ever loved."

"Shame."

"What?"

"If you'd babbled something stupid about admiring her, I would've been super mean."

"And I let the chance slip by!"

A shiver ran down his spine. He'd come incredibly close to stepping on a land mine.

"So I'll accept that for now," she said.

"Oh? Not gonna ask what you are to me?"

"Just how big a pain in the ass do you think I am?"

She gave him a look like she was totally willing to go there if he insisted, but he decided to beat a hasty retreat. No need to sour her mood if she was in a better one.

"So what did you want to talk about?"

"Not in the mood anymore," she said.

Maybe she was still a little grumpy.

"Aww. You said I should expect great things! I really was!"

"And whose fault is that?"

"I regret everything."

"Really?"

"From the bottom of my heart."

Mai laughed. Maybe she'd forgiven him? But no, it was a trap, lulling him into a false sense of security.

"Did you hold a mock wedding at this chapel?" she asked with a smile.

A fastball that would even shock the dual threat from the north.

"I thought you said you'd accept it for now?"

"......"

Her glare was terrifying.

"Uh, so she did try on a wedding dress."

His voice got very quiet.

"And was Shouko a portrait of loveliness?"

What was the right answer to that? He felt like any answer he gave would be wrong. The moment the conversation had headed this way, he was doomed.

"I bet you'll look amazing in *your* wedding dress, Mai."

"Up to you whether you get to see that."

"I would love to."

"Then correct your behavior."

"Will do."

When he took this seriously, Mai let out a very long sigh. But this was vastly preferable to those silent glares.

"I wanted to talk about the twenty-fourth," she said.

"Mm?"

"Of December."

"Christmas Eve?"

"If filming goes well, I shouldn't have to work that evening."

Her voice was flat, sounding neither excited nor angry. Maybe a bit like she was stifling her feelings.

"You expecting to add any more work?"

"It's possible, but I did ask Ryouko to leave my schedule open."

Mai glanced toward him. Looking up through her lashes expectantly.

"And Kaede said she'd be staying with your grandparents, so…"

She trailed off. Their eyes met. She obviously wanted him to finish the thought, but he wanted her to say it.

"So?" he said.

"Let's make it a date," she said, clearly trying very hard not to sound embarrassed. Before he could point this out, she blurted, "How about the illumination show on Enoshima?"

"……"

He couldn't answer immediately. He was too busy being surprised by multiple things at once.

First, just like Shouko had said, they were going to have a date.

And second, both potential dates were in the same place.

He had no way of knowing if Shouko had picked that spot in full knowledge of this fact, but it seemed likely she had.

"Sakuta?"

"The jellyfish at the aquarium might be better."

"The thing from the train ads?"

The aquarium was a short walk from Katase-Enoshima Station, and in recent years, they'd started putting lights in the jellyfish tank for the holidays and were advertising it heavily.

"Yes, that. Kept seeing the ads and got curious."

"Sakuta, do you even like jellyfish?"

"I think I would if I saw them with you."

"Ah. So an aquarium date, then. I'll be going straight there from work, so…meeting outside the aquarium should attract less attention than the station."

"Probably, yeah. But if you put in any kind of effort for my sake, you'll attract attention no matter where you are."

"Then definitely in front of the aquarium," Mai said, laughing off his attempt at baiting her. Mai knew perfectly well she could easily surpass his highest expectations. That was what she did. "Will six work?"

"I, uh…"

He hesitated, remembering what Shouko had said. She would also be waiting for him at six.

But that wasn't a reason to change the time.

It was Sakuta's job to choose. Following up on that choice was the only thing he could do here. Even if the day arrived and he felt conflicted or guilty, at six o'clock on December 24, he would be standing in front of the aquarium. When Mai arrived, he'd compliment her outfit, and they'd go see the lit-up jellyfish, say, "Kind of gross, but also beautiful," and enjoy their date as couples do.

That was what Sakuta could do. The only thing he could do for Mai, and for Shouko.

"Then I'll see you at six?" Mai said.

"Yes," he said firmly.

He loved Mai. She was the one who mattered most. That was all the reason he needed.

"I can't wait to see what present you get me!"

"Oh, so the date isn't good enough?"

They'd reached the residential area, so their voices were lower now. Mai had her head down, blushing a bit, not quite meeting his eye, but they kept the banter going all the way back home.

4

"Wait, why are you here, senpai?"

It was Sunday, December 14. Sakuta had come in to work, changed into his server uniform, and hit the floor, where he ran into the petite devil.

"Did you have a shift today?" she asked, shooting him a baffled look.

Tomoe Koga was a first-year student at his high school. She had short, fluffed-out hair and wore light makeup that was very "modern schoolgirl." A good match for the cuteness of the girls' uniforms here. He'd heard more than a few male customers talking about how cute she was.

"Replacing Kunimi."

"There is no way you could ever do *that*."

She clearly meant this.

"You know that one older lady who works here sometimes? She just looked at me and shook her head, saying, 'I was hoping it would be Yuuma,' so…cut me some slack."

Sakuta had not expected Yuuma to conquer the silver-haired staff, too, but neither age nor gender could escape the gravitational pull of his gentle smile. It was so not fair.

"I just assumed you didn't have enough money to buy Sakurajima a Christmas present and were loading up on shifts as a result."

"That wouldn't get me the money in time."

"I didn't say it was a good plan."

"How dumb do you think I am?"

"Do you have a present for her yet?"

"No money to buy one."

"Oh my *God*."

There'd been a series of unexpected expenses. That surprise trip to Kanazawa had really hurt. His paycheck had been deposited on the tenth, and nearly all of it had gone to paying back what Mai had lent him. And now he was going to have to pay for Kaede's makeover. There was nothing left to spend on a Christmas gift.

"Say, Koga…"

"I'm not giving you anything."

She was way ahead of him. And she'd said *giving* instead of *lending*. She knew him too well.

"Stingy."

"You're gonna end up tied to Mai's apron strings," she said, rolling her eyes.

"That's my superstring theory."

"Your what?"

"I see advanced physics jokes are beyond you."

"As if *you* understand them."

"I know I never will, which is all I really need to understand."

Once, he'd flipped through a book Rio was reading when he stopped by the science lab, but he hadn't even been able to follow the basic premise. Actually, he hadn't even made it that far—he'd started reading a passage marked "Before We Begin," made it halfway through the page, and quietly closed the book.

Leave the tricky subjects to the smart people. He just had to focus on things he could actually do. It had been an important life lesson.

He needed to focus not on unraveling superstring theory and

understanding the nature of the universe, but on how to get through a Christmas Eve in which both Mai and Shouko had asked him out. He'd made his choice there and would just have to act accordingly.

And since his mind was made up, nothing mattered more than looking forward to enjoying that date with Mai. Unreservedly.

"Did you get good news or something?"

"Huh?"

"You're grinning. And usually this is where you call me cheeky and then start harassing me."

"I do not."

Tomoe was really perceptive about these things. She kept a close eye on everyone around her and picked up on changes fast. If she was asking a question like that, it was a good sign. If he looked like good things were happening, that meant he really did feel like they were.

Here he was, caught in a dilemma, forced to make an impossible choice—but that wasn't so tragic after all. One was his current girlfriend, and the other his first love. It was ridiculous to agonize over it.

Christmas Eve was a special day that came only once a year. Especially for couples. And there were two girls who said they wanted to spend that day with him. How lucky was that?

"Something going on with you?"

"Huh? Why?"

"Your upper arms are thicker."

"They are not!"

"Oh, they were always like this?"

"You're so mean!"

Tomoe hugged herself and turned aside, shielding her arms from view.

"You're terribad! Terridactyl bad!"

"Welp, enough chitchat! Time for work!"

"I'm gonna lose weight and make you say sorry!"

"If you do, I'll treat you to a parfait."

They had a special going for a jumbo-sized strawberry-laden calorie bomb of a parfait. Tomoe would *love* it.

"Then I'd be fat again!"

He lived to please.

Sakuta worked his shift, stopping only to tease Tomoe, and punched out twenty minutes after the scheduled five o'clock end time. Just as he'd been about to go, a large party had rolled in, and they'd been busy getting their orders taken and delivered.

He changed back into street clothes, and by the time he left the restaurant, it was five thirty. Sakuta set off for the hospital where Shouko was staying, on foot.

He got caught in a sudden shower on the way and barely made it in the doors before visiting hours ended—it was 5:55. You couldn't exactly run in the hospital, so he headed to her room at a normal walking pace.

As he passed the nurses' station, he bowed his head. They all knew him by sight now.

"You've only got three minutes!" one of them said. The rules were the rules. But from the look in her eye, they were prepared to bend them a bit. "Hurry!"

Sakuta bobbed his head again and went straight on down the hall. Her room was up ahead. He could see the door.

He was still a good ten yards away from it when it opened a crack. A head poked out and peered down the hall—Shouko. She looked worried, but when she saw Sakuta walking toward her, she let out a cry, and a huge smile bloomed on her face.

"Sorry I'm late."

"N-no, you're early!" Not an accurate response.

"That's not even close to being true. Visiting hours are almost over."

"Early and late are minor details. What matters is that you came."

She flung the door open, waving him in. Her voice and expression were cheery, but she was pushing an IV stand around and wasn't exactly spry on her feet.

"......"

She really wasn't doing well.

"Hokay," Shouko grunted, heaving herself back into bed. Sakuta wasn't sure if it was a result of her condition or the long hospital stay, but she was noticeably deteriorating physically. Her pajamas seemed much baggier.

He took his perch on the stool and scanned the room's interior. Looking at Shouko was making his spirits flag. He noticed a familiar homework assignment on the bedside table and reached for it.

"Ah!"

For a moment, Shouko seemed upset. Like he'd seen something he shouldn't have, but he'd already seen this. The Future Schedule she'd written in grade school. And hadn't been able to complete, so she'd taken it home...

He opened it up and glanced down at the page.

"Hmm?"

This noise was prompted by a new note that hadn't been there a few days before.

Agree to a big date on Christmas Eve.

This had been added to the college student section.

Like the others, it appeared to have been there all along. What was going on here?

The day the older Shouko had made her shocking confession, Sakuta had asked her about this piece of paper. They'd figured her pulling a prank was the most likely explanation for it. But she denied everything.

"What would be the point of me doing something like that?"

Fair enough, he thought. This printout was always in the hospital room, and if big Shouko wanted to add something to it, she'd have to sneak in there somehow. Getting in and out multiple times without anyone spotting her would require skills like a movie spy.

He'd talked to Rio as well, but she'd just said, "I don't really know," and thrown her hands up. But she *had* said that big Shouko's actions were almost certainly connected—based purely on what was being added. Sakuta had reached the same conclusion.

"Another new entry," he said.

"Y-yes. It's still happening..."

Shouko was acting like that was a bad thing. She was staring at her hands, clearly not wanting to talk about the schedule assignment. As he wondered why, there was a knock at the door.

"Yes?" Shouko said, and the nurse poked her head in. The same one from earlier.

"I'm going to make the rounds and check the other rooms. You've got until then," she announced.

This was a roundabout way of telling them visiting hours were over. The clock showed it was after six.

"Then by all means, take your time."

"Afraid I can't do that," she said, laughing.

The nurse headed off down the hall. She did, indeed, move at the exact same speed she always did.

"I'll try to get here earlier tomorrow."

"Uh, about that, Sakuta..."

Shouko trailed off, a shadow passing over her face. She hung her head, her gaze fixed on her hands.

"Hmm?"

"I... I've known for a while I had to tell you, but..."

The anxious look in her eyes meant he could guess what this was about, and he was probably right.

"My condition...isn't good."

Her voice was quiet but clear. He could sense her desire to communicate this properly.

"......"

"By which I mean...it's pretty bad."

It felt like someone had attached a weight to his heart. Like his whole body was sinking into the floor.

"Mm," he managed.

"The medicine they're giving me is helping me manage for now, but...that can't go on forever."

"Yeah..."

"So, uh..."

As if summoning all her courage, Shouko cleared her throat and looked him right in the eye. Then she took a deep breath, eyes burning with resolve.

"Don't come to see me anymore," she said with a smile.

A bright, sunny smile. It was so picture perfect most would think she didn't have a care in the world.

How much courage did Shouko's little body have stuffed inside it? She must be scared to death. How could she find it in herself to worry about him?

Shouko was forced to say good-bye with a smile because she was thinking of him. The more he met her, the greater—and deeper—his grief would be when she was really gone. There was no way for them to go back to being strangers, but she was saying this in the hopes of lessening his pain in any way she could. Worrying only about what would happen to him once she was no longer here. This frail, tiny little girl...still only in her first year of junior high.

How could Shouko manage to shoulder so much all by herself? The world wasn't fair. It was so messed up, it wasn't even worth grumbling about.

But that made Sakuta's answer all the more obvious. He could leave the hard questions to the smart people. He just had to do the things he *could* do. Even here, there was something he could do. Something he could understand without needing to study.

He took a silent breath. Then he said, "Nah."

Just like he always did. With those same listless, dead eyes. No trace of enthusiasm in his voice. As if they were making routine small talk.

"Huh?" Shouko blinked at him. He didn't blame her. She'd summoned a lifetime of courage, and he'd dismissed it out of hand.

"I'll be here tomorrow and the day after," he said before she could recover. "Maybe there will be a few days when work keeps me away, but otherwise I'll be here every day until you get out."

If big Shouko hadn't told him what the future held, he might not have been capable of responding this way.

But she'd also said he came to see her every day. *That* Sakuta hadn't known the future, and he'd done it anyway. And Sakuta knew the future, so there was no way he was gonna do any less.

"But I..." Shouko's voice shook. "I—!"

She was still trying to argue with him.

"It's fine," he said, slowly getting to his feet. He took a step closer to the bed and put one hand on her head. "Makinohara, you did great."

"...Um?"

She blinked up at him, clearly not sure what that meant.

"You did great!"

Not letting her fears show on her face.

"You really hung in there."

Doing everything she could to keep her parents from worrying.

"You've worked so hard."

She must have been terrified, but she smiled brightly, thanked everyone, and did everything in her power to let them know how happy she'd been.

"All this time, you've been working harder than anyone."

She'd smiled every time he came to see her. Even today.

"...Sakuta," she said, her eyes filling with tears. She was undoubtedly trying to fight them back. Stop them spilling over. So she could keep on being happy Shouko Makinohara, loved by everyone.

And there was no way Sakuta was going to let her. Shouko deserved better. If she didn't get it, it was the world that was wrong.

"So you don't have to anymore."

This made her tears well up again.

"But…I…I…" Her voice shook. The next words stuck in her throat.

"You don't have to work so damn hard."

"!"

Her body shook.

"I… I want…"

She screwed up her eyes. Big tears struck the sheets, and the levees could no longer hold back the surging wave of her emotions.

"I never wanted to be sick!"

Her true feelings, out in the open at last. No one would dream of criticizing her for it. The tears flowed free, and she threw her arms around him, burying her face in his chest.

"I wanted to be like everyone else," she sobbed.

"Mm-hmm."

"Why did it have to be me?"

"Exactly."

"I want to live…"

"……"

"I want to live, too!"

"Yeah."

"To live and…and…"

All this time, Shouko had been unable to let these feelings out. Hadn't let herself do that. It would upset the grown-ups around her. Make them sad. Make her a burden, a problem. So…

"I just… I…"

"……"

"I want…"

Her voice was too choked with sobs for words to form. But these weren't feelings that could be expressed in words. Some could only be expressed in tears. Could only take the form of sobs. Feelings too strong and powerful to come out any other way. Her hands clutched his clothes, shaking and telling him more than mere words ever could.

"I don't..."

"I'll be fine."

"......"

"I'll be here tomorrow."

"...Sakuta."

"And the day after."

She let out a ragged gasp, trying to stop herself from sobbing.

"Maybe there will be a few days when work keeps me away."

"......"

"But otherwise I'll be here every day until you get out."

"...Really?"

Her voice was hoarse. With her nose clogged up, she sounded much younger than usual.

"Really."

"...Sakuta."

She was still sniffling a little, but she managed to let go of him.

"...You promise?"

"I do."

"Pinkie swear?"

Shouko held up her little hand. Sakuta hooked his pinkie around hers.

"This is more awkward than I thought," she said, smiling sheepishly. Like she was trying to hide just how much it was really getting to her.

Sakuta plucked two tissues from the box on the side table and handed them to her. He'd meant for her to dry her tears, but she blew her nose instead.

This made him laugh out loud.

"What?" she said, blinking up at him. When he said nothing, she started laughing, too.

Even if just for that one moment, he hoped her fears were banished.

If Sakuta had managed that feat, he'd done a decent job. He'd be thoroughly satisfied with his accomplishments.

"Okay, visiting hours are over!" the nurse said, like she'd been waiting for the right moment. Her voice had an "acting" quality to it, so perhaps she'd been listening from outside. From the look she gave him, she definitely had. That was definitely a "Well done" look.

"Okay, see you tomorrow."

"Yes!" Shouko said, and she waved good-bye with a smile.

He raised a hand to wave back, and as he did…

"……!"

…she let out a little gasp, and a shadow passed over her face. Both hands snapped to her chest, squeezing tight like she was fighting something back.

Then she toppled over on the bed, writhing in pain.

Her lips moved like she was trying to say something, but only a rasp came out. This all happened in mere seconds.

"Move aside!" the nurse said, pushing Sakuta out of the way and hitting the nurse call button.

"What is it?" came a voice from the speaker.

"Sudden change in Makinohara's condition," she said, her voice calm.

Then she called Shouko's name a few times, trying to get a response.

As she did, two doctors in white coats came rushing in. They were maybe midforties and midthirties, respectively. Three nurses came after them. The hospital room was now swarming with medical staff.

There was no room for Sakuta near the bed, and he ended up with his back pressed up against the far wall.

The older doctor quickly examined Shouko and said, "Secure an operating room and call her family. She needs to be moved to the ICU." Two nurses ran out, and another nurse came in with a stretcher.

Following the doctor's instructions, they moved Shouko's tiny body onto the stretcher and hustled her out of the room.

It all unfolded at dizzying speeds. Sakuta could do nothing but stand there and watch. A normal high school kid couldn't help here. Doing nothing was all he could do. But doing nothing made him anxious, which led to panic and then outright fear.

Doing nothing was destroying him. He knew Shouko would get her transplant and be saved. But even with that knowledge, the tension in the room was so great, it felt like a vise was tightening around him. He couldn't stop himself from wondering if Shouko had been wrong and the future she'd promised might not come. Sakuta had never seen anyone writhing in pain like Shouko had, and it left him with a storm of emotions raging inside.

Without really thinking, he took a step toward the hall to follow her stretcher.

He made it a couple of steps, but as he took a third, a sudden pain shot across his chest. It raced from the inside out.

"...Owww," he groaned. He'd almost passed out from the first wave, but he somehow held on. His vision narrowed. Sound drained away. Unable to stand upright, he staggered, leaning against the wall of the corridor. Then he slid down it and collapsed on the floor in a ball.

There was something on the hand that had clutched his chest. Something unpleasant, something *wrong*. He looked down and saw red. Fresh blood was seeping through his shirt.

He managed to lift his head enough to see Shouko's stretcher disappearing down the hall. But he couldn't hear the wheels squeaking or the doctors and nurses talking. The ache in his chest was all he could feel. It snatched everything else away from him.

"What's going on...?"

The pain dominating his mind infuriated and baffled him.

The scars on his chest were a sign of his regrets and inadequacy two years ago, when he'd failed to save Kaede. He'd always imagined his Adolescence Syndrome had arrived to punish him for failing to save his sister.

"Then why now?"

He didn't know.

What was happening at the hospital had nothing to do with Kaede—either Kaede. Shouko's attack had obviously come as a shock, but…he knew she would survive. Big Shouko had told him what the future had in store. Either way, it was too early to start regretting anything.

So…

"…Why?"

He didn't get it.

But the pain was telling him something else.

Maybe he'd been very wrong.

Maybe the scars on his chest weren't what he'd originally thought.

With that possibility whispering in the back of his mind, Sakuta's consciousness faded, and the world went black.

5

He heard lapping waves in the distance.

The sound came closer, rising toward his feet, like the ocean's very existence was seeping into the fabric of his entire body.

The waves crested inches from his toes and pulled away.

When he finally registered what he was seeing, Sakuta realized he was standing on the beach.

The familiar sights of Shichirigahama. Enoshima a silhouette against the red sky of sunset. The sea breeze felt good. The surf surprisingly loud. All of it felt very *real.*

But this was a dream.

Somehow he knew that.

He'd been having these dreams less often. Dreams of two years ago, when he met high school Shouko.

This was one of them. As proof of that, he heard her voice.

"Wanna kiss?"

Big Shouko was standing three steps away. In a Minegahara uniform, just as she had two years ago. Little Shouko, now in high school.

"No thanks," he said curtly.

"Don't worry—I brushed my teeth."

"They taught me in grade school you shouldn't kiss total strangers."

"They didn't teach *me* that."

"Yeah, me either."

"Heh-heh, then why say they did?"

They were laughing together.

"But, Sakuta…"

"What?"

"Did I make your heart race?"

There was a triumphant smile on her face. Delighting in tormenting junior high Sakuta.

"It makes the wounds on my chest throb, so don't get me too worked up."

"You got worked up because a total stranger asked you to kiss?"

"……"

"That's a little strange."

Shouko leaned forward a bit so she could look up at him. The wind caught her hair, and it spilled off her shoulders.

"It's a basic male response."

"Is that all?"

She was being very persistent.

"That's all."

"And yet you come to see me almost every day."

"I come to see the ocean."

"Oh?"

"What are you driving at?"

"I wanna make you say it."

"……"

"Okay, fine," she said, sticking out her tongue. "I am, too," she added, like it was a big deal.

"You are what?"

"Getting worked up because I'm with you."

She had an impish grin that suggested she knew exactly what she was doing, but Sakuta's heart still leaped out of his chest.

"Seriously, quit making my wounds hurt. If they start bleeding again, I can't tell anyone why, and it's a real problem."

Just to be sure, he took a look down his shirt. The telltale gouges were still covered in scabs, healing. Red, but not bleeding.

"You're fine."

"……"

How would she know? He almost snapped at her. But he couldn't do that. There was an unmistakable tenderness in her voice. She was trying to reassure him. And she sounded weirdly confident as well. At the very least, Shouko believed he really was fine. She wouldn't say it like that otherwise.

"You'll get better."

Her voice came right next to his ear, warming his entire body.

"Yeah, I mean…eventually."

It would be bad otherwise. But Shouko shook her head. Twice, quietly.

"The wounds in your heart and on your chest? I'll heal both of them."

Her smile was far too gentle. It was like being wrapped in the warmth of the spring sun.

He caught himself staring and awkwardly tore his eyes away.

"What does that even *mean*?" he muttered.

So he didn't notice.

"You'll be fine. I'll be there for you."

This sounded a lot like what she'd said before, so Sakuta didn't realize what she meant.

He just focused on trying to calm his racing heart. Hanging on for dear life and trying to slow it down.

* * *

When his eyes opened, a white ceiling was staring impassively down at him.

Long fluorescent lights.

When he was sure this was reality and that he was on a hospital bed, the pain in his chest throbbed. He looked down and found himself wrapped in a slew of bandages.

He remembered passing out. Crumpling over from the pain in the hall, and the next thing he knew, he was here.

"Sakuta," a voice said. Shouko leaned in from the side of the bed. Big Shouko. Wearing glasses and a knit hat. Sakuta's head was strangely clear, and he could tell right away this was a disguise she'd donned to slip into the hospital unnoticed.

"You're in the hospital. You remember that?"

"...Yeah."

"I got a call saying you suddenly collapsed... You gave me quite a fright."

"......"

She looked worried, but he just stared at her without a word.

"Sakuta?"

His hand moved to the bandages on his chest.

"I had a dream."

"You did?"

"About two years ago..."

"......"

"Around when I first met you."

"Oh..."

"Same thing was happening then."

"......"

"The wounds had opened on my chest, and..."

Sakuta was choosing his words carefully, his thoughts circling, but he was oddly certain he was closing in on an answer.

He'd realized something but wasn't conscious of it yet. But he'd accepted what his body was telling him. All this time, he'd been sure the wounds were caused by Kaede's bullying and the regret that he hadn't protected her, a way of punishing himself for his inability to act. The time lines had added up, and he'd been only too well aware of how distraught he'd been. There'd been no evidence to contradict that theory. It had simply seemed to be the most likely explanation.

But it didn't explain the changes in him over the last few days. Certainly, Shouko's deterioration had affected him, but he knew she would be saved. So why had the wounds on his chest reopened?

Two years ago, he'd met Shouko not long after they first appeared.

Two years later, when he'd been grieving the loss of hiragana Kaede, they'd opened again. But that was probably just a coincidence. Who had he met moments later?

"......"

The woman warmly watching over him.

Sakuta was already sure no other answer fit. His body was screaming it at him. His very pulse bellowing.

So he spoke without surprise, confusion, fear, anxiety, or the slightest trace of hope.

"It's my heart that's inside you, isn't it?"

"......"

Shouko's eyes slowly closed. And then she nodded slightly, confirming it.

"I thought you'd figure it out," she said. She put her hands to her chest. "You gave me a future."

Her eyes were glistening. Quite a lot of conflicted emotions there. Gratitude, but also heartbreak and grief. All these feelings tangled together, so mixed up it was impossible to tell where each one began.

"......"

"......"

Neither knew what to say next.

Then there was a noise coming from the hall.

"......?"

Both turned toward the door.
"Oh…," Sakuta said.
Mai was standing there. White as a sheet.
"What does that mean?" she asked, her voice trembling.
Her words echoed quietly through the hospital room.

TWO Paths

1

Three respective silences filled the air.

One belonged to Sakuta. Another to grown-up Shouko. And the last was Mai's.

The palpable silence was finally broken by Mai's footsteps. She crossed the room, moving over to Sakuta's bed. She looked at him first, then turned to Shouko.

"You mean…?" she started.

"……"

How should he answer? How should he respond? He wasn't at all sure. It was plainly not a situation he could worm out of or insist was insignificant. All three of them could feel the tension in the air, which was why the silence was so intense. You could cut the tension with a knife.

Then Shouko exhaled. Very deliberately. Both turned to look at her.

"Ten days from now," she began.

Had she realized there was no getting out of this, or had she always meant to tell Mai? Shouko certainly seemed to be taking it in stride.

"December twenty-fourth."

That was Christmas Eve. Not that far in the future.

"It'll be the coldest day all winter, and like the weather reports promise, it'll start to snow come afternoon. So much snow it sticks, even this far south."

There was an open question in Mai's eyes, but she said nothing. She didn't want to interrupt. No matter how many doubts this speech raised, she was choosing to hear Shouko out first.

"Sakuta promises to meet you for a date, and on his way there...a car skids on some ice."

Shouko was describing events that hadn't happened yet like they already had. Her words held neither hope nor despair. They were a plain statement of fact. Nothing more, nothing less. This was simply what Shouko knew to be true, the natural progression of events in her reality. Shouko was from six or seven years in the future, and events taking place ten days from now were in the distant past for her.

"How do you know...?" Mai asked. The obvious question.

"Because I'm from the future."

Mai's brow furrowed briefly. She caught Shouko's eye, considered her words for a moment, and then turned to Sakuta.

"It's true," he said, nodding.

At the very least, she'd been right about Mai's and Kaede's Christmas plans. And Kaede's in particular was not something you could blindly guess.

Mai thought about this for a long moment.

"Okay...," she said.

"Sakuta is taken to the hospital but never comes to. Eventually, he's declared brain-dead."

He'd known as much from the moment he realized the truth, but hearing this from her carried a very different weight. It hit him hard.

Sakuta's hand moved to his chest.

"......"

He could feel his heart beating.

"They find an organ donor card among Sakuta's possessions. When he's declared brain-dead, they get permission from his family—or so I was told later."

When Mai said nothing, Sakuta let out a low noise. His throat was dry, and the sound caught in it.

What had gone through his father's mind when he got that call? Informed of his son's death, then moments later asked to approve the use of his organs?

There would have been no time to process his emotions. But his future father had respected Sakuta's wishes and approved the donorship.

Shouko was living proof of that. She'd received the transplant and was alive and healthy.

"Three days after the accident, on December twenty-seventh…I was in the ICU, kept alive thanks to a ventricular assist device. And miraculously, a donor heart arrived just in time."

Shouko put her hands to her chest again. Closing her eyes, as if listening closely to the heartbeat inside.

"……"

He didn't know what to ask. She'd already said everything he'd wanted to know. It had only taken a couple of minutes to relate the facts. The facts of Sakuta's death.

"And when you woke…?" he asked after some thought. Shouko had probably been asked this many times. But he'd chosen to ask it because it was a question his future self would not be able to ask her himself.

"When I woke up after the operation, none of it seemed real. The anesthetic was still in effect, and I fell asleep again in no time."

"……"

"But the next time I woke, I saw my mom's eyes red from crying, and I knew she'd been sobbing the whole time, and I was so happy, I cried, too."

"Good," he said, finding himself relieved to hear it.

"My father kept saying 'Thank goodness' over and over, and I was just so relieved. I could finally feel my own heartbeat."

"……"

"Ba-bump, ba-bump. The heart that saved me. It was always there…"

Her voice was choked with tears. The emotions of that moment came rushing back to her. More tears welled up in her eyes and spilled down her cheeks. She brushed them off with her fingers.

"I had no way of knowing who the donor was, then. I just kept repeating 'Thank you' again and again to whoever it was."

There was peace in her eyes. A wealth of kindness. This "Thank you" was clearly meant for Sakuta.

"I didn't start to suspect anything until the mandatory rest period ended, and I was transferred from the ICU to a regular room. Normally, you only find out who the donor is under extraordinary circumstances. But…"

In Shouko's case, those circumstances aligned. It wasn't even that dramatic. It was just simple logic.

"You found out because you knew me."

"Yeah," she whispered, nodding. "When I tried to call you to tell you about the operation, I couldn't get through. At first, I didn't know why, but…"

Shouko lifted her head and looked at Mai.

"…there was someone who'd seen everything," she said. A pained look on her face. "Mai told me everything. She said I'd find out eventually, if I tried to go see you."

"……"

Mai said nothing. This was something she didn't know yet. What must have been going through future Mai's head when she chose to tell Shouko the truth?

Sakuta had no idea. It was likely the current Mai didn't know, either.

"That's about all there is to say," Shouko concluded, looking rather sad. Considering the weight of what she had revealed, it had taken very few words. "That's the story of how Sakuta saved my life."

"……"

He had no words. Did it still not feel real? Or was something else washing over him? Either way, Sakuta couldn't bring himself to speak.

"......"

Mai seemed to be in the same condition. She wasn't meeting Sakuta's eye, or Shouko's. She was just staring absently at the bed frame.

"So for Christmas this year, I recommend you have a quiet date at home," Shouko said, her voice suddenly very cheerful.

If he stayed home and didn't go out, then there was no way he'd get hit by a car on the twenty-fourth. He'd never be taken to the hospital or declared brain-dead. And he wouldn't become Shouko's donor.

The future would change.

He'd have changed it.

The transplant Shouko should have received would never happen.

"Don't worry."

"But..."

"Little me still has time left. Have some faith in modern medicine."

"Says the time traveler..."

There was more he should have said. But he couldn't find the words to say it. He hadn't sorted through his own feelings at all.

Sakuta wasn't sure what was important, what he should protect, or what he should choose. How could he have anything to say to Shouko, who'd already accepted all of it?

"I'm sure another donor will come along."

Shouko's smile was like a warm hug. One that made him feel safe and secure.

"Right," she said, getting up from her stool. "Not safe to stay long in the same hospital as little me, so I'm gonna head on back."

"......"

"......"

Neither Sakuta nor Mai moved a muscle. Neither of them could respond at all.

"Mai," Shouko said.

"...Yes?"

"Look after Sakuta."

"I don't need you to tell me that," Mai said, but her voice shook.

"Maybe not!"

Shouko beamed back at her. Nothing about this was cheerful, but she looked like she'd accomplished a grand deed. Sakuta didn't realize what that meant. His head was spinning too fast to pick up on anything that nuanced. All he could do was watch her leave.

Sakuta and Mai settled the bills and paperwork, and they left the hospital about twenty minutes after Shouko.

Their only option had been to explain away the scars as an old wound that had reopened, but since the bleeding had subsided, the doctor they met with hadn't questioned them further.

Sakuta asked about little Shouko, but all he got was "We can't share much information, even if you are acquainted." But the doctor did let them know she was undergoing an operation to implant a device that would keep her heart beating. Sakuta was grateful for that information.

There was nothing he could accomplish by hanging around the hospital any longer. And if something brought the conversation back to the wounds on his chest, it could get awkward, so he headed to the entrance, where Mai was waiting.

"It all work out?" she asked.

"I wriggled out of it, yeah."

"Good."

With that, they left the hospital grounds.

"......"

"......"

For a long time, neither of them spoke.

But Sakuta assumed they were thinking about the same things. In fact, he was certain of it.

So when Mai suddenly said, "Then it's all true," he didn't have to ask what.

"Don't see why Shouko would lie about this."

"I wish she was."

"……"

They'd danced around it briefly but were soon back to silence.

They were walking slower than usual, their breaths visible in the cold air. It felt like they both needed the extra time. Needed this moment of quiet.

To understand the truth.

To accept the truth.

It took time and silence to process the reality of it.

Mai was so close their shoulders almost touched, and Sakuta could feel her there, but he kept his eyes straight ahead.

At last, without further conversation, they reached his apartment building.

Sakuta started to head in, then realized Mai had stopped behind him. He could feel her looking at him. So as he turned, he spoke first.

"Uh, Mai…"

He hadn't reached any kind of conclusion. In no way had his emotions caught up to the facts. He was just driven by an instinctive feeling that he had to be the first to speak. That he couldn't punt the choice of his life to her.

"Mai, um…"

He was definitely stalling. He didn't have anything to follow through with. He couldn't find any other words. He was drawing a blank. No, there was one thing. Somewhere at the back of his mind, he considered saying a definitive good-bye. It got as far as his throat, but he'd learned earlier that evening exactly what hearing that felt like, and he couldn't bring himself to do that.

——*"Don't come to see me anymore."*

Shouko had summoned all her courage to say that to him, and it had been brutal for both of them.

"Sakuta," Mai said when he hesitated.

He looked up, and her beautiful eyes were looking right at him.

"I'm not going to lose you."

"......"

He couldn't respond in any meaningful way, primarily because he was so stunned she'd read his hesitation that accurately. And she'd cut him off before he could do anything as stupid as asking her to forget him.

"We'll have to change our date plans, though."

"......"

"Nodoka has a Christmas concert, so she'll be out. We could hang out at my place, just the two of us. I'll be working all day, so I'll buy a big old Christmas cake on the way home."

Mai's voice seemed to be filling up the silent night air around them.

"For New Year's, we should visit the Tsurugaoka Hachimangu Shrine. The crowds will be intense on the first, so it might be better to do it after winter vacation ends."

"...Yeah."

"I'll also make some chocolate for you on Valentine's Day."

"...Mm."

"I'll be graduating in the spring, but...I do plan to make enough time to tutor you occasionally, so be prepared."

"Will you be wearing the bunny-girl outfit?"

"I'll put it on once you've been accepted to college."

"I can't wait."

On the surface, this was like all their interactions.

Their voices sounded bright and cheery.

But behind the words and smiles, Sakuta's heart was empty. They were talking about the happy moments the future would bring, but he felt nothing. It didn't seem as if they were talking about him. He felt no joy, pleasure, or happiness. Nor did he feel any anxiety, fear, or despair.

He was responding the right way, but those words didn't feel like they came from his own free will.

December 24. Christmas Eve. Sakuta would die in a car accident on his way to a date with Mai.

He still hadn't come to terms with what Shouko had told them about the future. He knew he had only ten days left to live, but it still didn't feel like they were talking about his death. All he'd really understood was that he couldn't imagine himself dying.

"And a year after that, we'll start college together."

"......"

"So I want you to choose a future with me. That's my wish."

Mai's expression never changed. She held his gaze the whole time, only a faint trace of sadness in her eyes. Her voice never broke. She never got emotional. She was just calmly discussing their future together.

"I'm not gonna stay over tonight."

"Okay."

"I think that's probably best."

He needed time to think.

"You're right."

Sakuta and Mai both needed time. Especially because they knew they had so little left.

"Okay. Good night, then." Mai waved good-bye.

"Yeah. Good night," he said.

Mai went into the building across the street, and Sakuta watched her go.

She didn't look back. Didn't stop to give him one last impish grin or wave a second time.

When she was out of sight, Sakuta looked up at the sky and let out a long white breath.

"......"

But he said nothing at all.

2

The teacher stood at the blackboard, going over the English problems on the final exam. Nobody was paying much attention—vacation was too close at hand.

Their test sheets had come back, and some students were scowling at the scores, while others played with their phones under their desks.

Sakuta noted all this out of the corner of his eye but was also diligently taking notes. Making sure to write down the correct answers to everything he'd gotten wrong. In actuality, there weren't that many. The number *82* was dancing at the top of his exam sheet. This was Nodoka's doing. She'd taught him well, despite all her grumbling. But despite a record high grade, Sakuta didn't take any real pleasure in it.

Four days had already gone by.

Four mornings since Sakuta had keeled over from the wounds on his chest.

That much time has passed since he'd learned he would get run over by a car on Christmas Eve.

It was now December 18. A Thursday.

Less than a week until his fate was sealed.

He was technically aware the date was approaching, but the concept still didn't feel real to him. And that left him unsure what to do—so he just went through the motions of his daily routine.

Get up in the morning, get ready, go to school.

Sit through classes.

When those ended, go home. If he had a shift, work the hours he was scheduled for. If Tomoe was working, too, he'd tease her a bit to let off steam.

When night fell, he'd go to sleep and wake up in the morning. And then repeat the whole cycle.

He didn't do a single extraordinary thing.

He was still stopping by to see Shouko after school, but she was confined to the ICU. Only her family could see her there, so he was mostly visiting an empty room.

Room 301, the one Shouko had been in. She was no longer on that bed. Her schoolbooks and notes were still there, as was the box of snacks Sakuta had brought her from Kanazawa. A shroud of sadness hung over the room. When Shouko had still been there, she'd given the place warmth and light, but now it felt sterile. Like time had stopped.

But yesterday—Wednesday—he'd popped in after work and happened to run into Shouko's mother. She told him the surgery to prolong her life had been a success. Just as big Shouko had promised. The procedure had implanted a device that would keep her heart beating. He couldn't bring himself to say "Good," so he simply said "I'll come again" before she could do the polite thing and tell him not to.

Well aware of Sakuta's actions, big Shouko was still hanging out at his place. She'd wake him up when he overslept, make dinner, see him off, and welcome him back home. She really hadn't changed at all. Like she was completely at peace. He had no clue how that was possible.

He'd barely spoken to Mai since then. They weren't actively avoiding each other, but Mai's schedule left them with little time to sit down together. In a certain light, this could be seen as Mai going through her routine, the same way Sakuta was his. Her schedule couldn't be changed as easily. The famous "Mai Sakurajima" had a lot riding on her work. And Sakuta knew perfectly well how much Mai valued living up to that.

He'd forced her to tell him her thoughts on his future. Made her say those awful words.

——*"I want you to choose a future with me. That's my wish."*

The ball was back in Sakuta's court. He was holding it gingerly in both hands. Showing no signs of tossing it back.

"……"

He realized he'd stopped taking notes.

"I'm sure none of you are in the mood, but reviewing your results is important," their English teacher advised.

Sakuta looked up. The teacher had finished explaining the final essay and was brushing the chalk off his hands. Then the bell rang—fourth period was over. They had only morning classes this week, so classes were done for the day.

A few minutes later, the end-of-day homeroom began but concluded soon after, with nothing of importance discussed.

Sakuta picked up his bag, intending to stop by the hospital again. But as he stepped into the hall, someone grabbed his shoulder.

"Hey! Azusagawa!"

He turned his head to look and found Saki Kamisato glaring up at him. She had both hands on her hips like she was furious.

"What?"

"You're on cleaning duty! You've skipped out three days in a row, so today you're doing it all on your own!"

He checked the cleaning duty schedule. Saki was right. They were at the top of the alphabet.

He'd been too caught up in what was coming to realize he was ditching everyone.

"Sorry. I'll make sure to handle it today."

He put his bag back on his desk and opened the cleaning locker at the back. He took out the push broom and started sweeping trash toward the front of the room.

"Hey."

He looked up and saw that Saki had followed him. She still looked angry.

"What?"

"Why didn't you argue?"

"Huh?"

"Are you nuts?"

"I'm in the wrong here. And this was *your* idea."

It seemed like a fair punishment for skipping three days. He didn't see why he'd argue the point.

"Still!"

He had no idea what her problem was, but Saki was in a very bad mood.

"You and Kunimi having problems or something?"

"We're doing fine."

"Good, good. I wish you everlasting happiness," he said in a totally normal tone of voice. He started sweeping again.

"Oh?"

That "Oh?" sounded irate. Had he said or done anything to provoke that?

"You know you oppose me dating him."

Getting involved in this seemed like trouble, so he just kept cleaning.

"Oh, what's the point?"

What *was* the point?

"Are you even listening?"

He considered ignoring her again, but he figured it would make her even more furious, so he gave up.

"I'm not opposed to anything. I'm sure you've got some attractive qualities I've just failed to perceive."

"What does that even mean?"

"When I hear Kunimi talk about you, I can tell he really does love you."

"……"

Saki was still glaring at him angrily, but she'd stopped putting that rage into words. Maybe he'd gotten through to her a bit. At least, he hoped so.

"You take the window side."

"Huh?"

When he glanced up, he found her taking out another broom. She ignored his questioning look and started sweeping the hallway side of the room.

"What are you doing, Kamisato?"

"Cleaning."

He could see that.

"Why?"

"I'm also on cleaning duty."

"……"

This was ridiculous. They couldn't even begin to communicate. But by all appearances, she'd decided to help, so he might as well accept her generosity.

"Uh, Kamisato."

"……"

Saki didn't even bother glancing his way. She was cleaning industriously, her butt pointed his way.

"I don't want Kunimi killing me, so maybe don't bend over that far in front of me."

She instantly realized what he was getting at and snapped a hand to the back of her skirt. She swung around, looking furious.

"Drop dead!"

All he'd seen was gym shorts, so he thought this was a bit uncalled for.

"I plan to. Don't worry."

The words came out before he could stop them.

"What did you just say?"

At least he'd said it too quietly for her to hear.

"I said thanks for helping."

Saki paused, and their eyes met. She soon looked away.

"D-don't be ridiculous," she whispered. Weirdly embarrassed. She quickly turned her back and started sweeping again.

"What was that?"

"I said drop dead!"

"Oh, right, right."

He was smirking a bit. Not because Saki's attitude was making him laugh, but because he was having a conversation like this, despite everything. And that struck him as funny. He'd learned what fate had in store for him and then immediately afterward had seen a whole new side of someone he'd always struggled with. How could he not laugh?

Even with two of them cleaning, the classroom was pretty big. It took three times as long as it usually would. Which made sense, since there were usually three times this many people on duty. If he'd been on his own, it would have taken even longer. He was definitely grateful for the help.

A full half hour after homeroom ended, the school's ambiance had shifted right from "after class" to "club time."

Not something Sakuta dealt with often, so he changed into his shoes and fled the building, making a beeline toward the gates.

But on the way, he heard a sound that made him stop. The rhythmic noise of a ball bouncing. A big, heavy ball. It came from the gym.

He wouldn't normally have paid it any attention, but today something made him turn and head over to the gym doors.

The metal doors leading directly into the gym itself were standing open, and he had a clear view of the interior. A group of first-year girls were hanging around. "Kunimi is so cool!" "But he's going out with Kamisato, right?" "Even if they broke up, he'd never look at *you*."

The boy they were talking about was busy warming up, dribbling two balls at once.

Sakuta watched for a bit. Eventually, Yuuma noticed and looked up. Their eyes met. Yuuma briefly frowned, then took a shot with one ball and came over, dribbling the other. The first ball sailed smoothly across the court and passed right through the hoop. It didn't even graze the rim. Just a soft little *poof* as the net swished. The girls all squealed.

"What's up?"

"What's up with you, Kunimi?"

"Huh?"

"Just how popular are you aiming to be?"

"You're the one dating Sakurajima," Yuuma cackled.

"Well, Mai *is* the cutest."

"So you're just here to brag?"

"Obviously not."

"Then seriously, why are you here?"

Yuuma spun the ball on his finger.

"Just came to see you."

"Aw, are you my girlfriend now?"

"Kamisato says shit like that?"

"She can be real charming, you know?"

Yuuma knew she and Sakuta didn't get along, so he made a habit of regularly extolling her praises. He seemed to want his friends and girlfriend to get along.

"Speaking of her…"

If he didn't give some reason for being here, Yuuma was gonna keep asking.

"What about her?"

"She helped me clean. Tell her thanks again for me, will you?"

"I'm lost."

"If you wanna know more, take time out of your busy flirting schedule and have her tell you."

"I mean, I planned to."

"That's all."

Sakuta turned and started walking away.

"Sakuta," Yuuma called after him.

Sakuta looked over his shoulder.

"See you later."

A standard thing to say when you parted. An ordinary phrase with a promise to meet again built in.

"……"

Sakuta answered with a look. Not a "Sure" or a "Later." He couldn't even manage that much.

They had school again tomorrow. They might even pull a shift together at work. This wasn't likely to be the last time they met, so why not say it?

But he didn't respond. There was a clear reluctance to do so inside him. Somewhere along the line, his fear of the future had ballooned up within him.

"Not funny," he muttered as he headed out the gate.

The warning bells were ringing at the railroad crossing. Sakuta stopped to wait, examining the emotions that were driving him.

Maybe this was the same feeling that had made him turn toward the sound of the basketball. A sudden urge to go see his friend.

Deep inside, the notion that there might not be another chance was gnawing at him. On an instinctual level.

It was obvious why.

He'd thought he was fretting about which choice to make, but over the last four days, the scale within him had tipped. Tipped without him realizing it.

And the thing that had finally made him aware of this was an ordinary conversation with a friend. That was all it took.

It didn't require anything dramatic. This was how the world was. There was no telling what would do the trick. This time it had been Yuuma. And that fact left Sakuta making a face.

A train from Kamakura, bound for Fujisawa, rolled through the crossing behind the lowered gates. Sakuta should be on that train, but running now wasn't gonna get him there in time.

The train headed off to his left, crossing a narrow river and coming to a halt beside a tiny station platform. The warning bells stopped, and the crossing gates lifted. It was quiet once again.

"Something good happen?"

The words came from right next to him. He knew that voice. He didn't even have to look.

"Futaba..."

Rio was standing beside him.

The sound of her approach had been drowned out by the warning bells, and he hadn't noticed at all.

"No club today?"

She normally holed up in the science lab after classes, doing experiments.

"I saw you out the window of the lab, so I took the day off."

That wasn't the reason he'd expected. He'd assumed something more prosaic, like the teacher who sponsored the club couldn't stay late.

"Is that a romantic confession?"

"I feel like you've been avoiding me."

"......"

This one was so unexpected, he forgot to respond at all. The gates had gone up ages ago, but he'd forgotten to cross, too.

He put that surprise into a look, staring at her from the side.

"Since the start of the week."

"You're imagining it."

He didn't think he could get out of having this conversation, but he put up a futile resistance. He certainly wasn't about to just give up and spill the beans.

This wasn't something he could get Rio's advice on. He had to choose between two lives. His own or Shouko's. That wasn't a burden he could dump on Rio.

And she already knew a lot of it, which was why he'd been consciously avoiding her. There was no telling what might give her the hint she needed to realize the whole truth.

It had been just a theory, but circumstantial evidence had already led Rio to the idea that Shouko was from the future. If she knew Sakuta's wounds were reacting funny, she might quickly realize they weren't caused by regret and powerlessness. And the moment things stopped adding up, Rio would begin to question her hypothesis.

"What happened?"

"Like I said, you're imagining this."

"I know you collapsed on Sunday."

"......"

"And that Shouko's in the ICU. I went to the hospital yesterday."

"Oh."

It was so like her to do the legwork first.

"Then you already know?" he asked, raising the white flag.

"I have arrived at a possible explanation."

She sounded disappointed. Like she'd really wanted her idea to be wrong. She'd wanted Sakuta to deny the whole thing.

"Every time your wounds open, Shouko appears."

She was staring straight ahead. At the waters of Shichirigahama. The view across the railroad crossing. The gentle slope running all the way down to the beach. It was less than one hundred yards away. The fastest man in the world could reach it in less than ten seconds.

"You're really something."

"The two Shoukos are likely unable to meet on a quantum level. Same as when there were two of me. I believe she only exists when she is being observed."

"But normally she only exists as a possibility?"

"Yes. Your beloved quantum physics. But you and Shouko *have* met. Even though a part of her is yours."

"......"

Rio was a constant source of astonishment. She seriously had worked it all out on her own.

"And because two copies of your heart can't naturally exist simultaneously, perhaps this is what causes the wounds on your chest. You're breaking the rules of the world, and the world is lashing out."

What could he do but laugh?

"You're incredible, Futaba."

"Your attitude clinched it for me."

"It did?"

"If you're avoiding me, you must have a significant reason to do so."

"Like I had a choice! I can't exactly come to you and go, 'Which should I choose?'"

But now he was opening up. Rio had made it so he could do so without pressure. Trying to maintain dignity would be a waste.

"I'll get hit by a car on the twenty-fourth."

Might as well put the date out there, too. If she knew this much, Rio deserved time to adjust and ready herself for what was coming.

"Sakurajima knows?"

The crossing bells began to ring again.

"She does. She was there when we heard."

"You've talked it over?"

"It was awful. I let her say her piece first."

He would have preferred to reach an answer before Mai did. But none had emerged. At the time, he'd thought his head was just spinning too fast, but maybe that wasn't true. In hindsight, he felt like he'd always known his answer. It had been there, deep down inside him—he just hadn't realized it.

And he'd said nothing because he knew the answer would break Mai's heart.

"This is all I can really say here," Rio said.

The crossing gates lifted again.

"But you should really talk to Mai. Properly."

"Yeah, I know."

"That's really all I can…" Rio's voice broke. Like it had caught on the back of her nose.

"But you're the only one who shows up to tell me these things, Futaba."

And he was more grateful for it than she could possibly know. Having a friend who would scold him for his indecision and weakness was invaluable.

"Azusagawa, I..."

The train pulled out of the nearby station and drowned out Rio's whisper. The noise of the warning bells made it impossible to hear more.

But he knew what she wanted to say. Rio was always logical, so if she was getting emotional, it meant only one thing.

She didn't want this.

Her could see her lips trembling. But she knew that anything she said would just put more pressure on him, so she stopped herself short. He could see tears falling behind her glasses.

The train chugged slowly past them. The sounds of the train and the crossing bells closed off the world, and Sakuta put his arms around her, pulling her head to his chest, as if trying to hide her tears.

"Sorry for not being Kunimi."

"Why are you like this? Even when..."

Her forehead pressed against him, she let out a wail—but that, too, was lost in the sounds of the railroad crossing.

3

He had to face Mai eventually.

Rio forced him to make up his mind on that account, but Mai got back really late that day, and on the Friday and Saturday that followed, she wasn't scheduled to come back at all, so he was unable to put this decision into action.

She called from the hotel in the evening, but all he did was report his exam grades.

"Sounds like I'll have to crack the stick harder next time."

"I tend to do better with the carrot."

Neither of them mentioned the twenty-fourth. He figured this meant they both knew they should talk about it in person.

And with the timing slipping away from him, the nerve he'd gathered up started scattering, too. Too many unnecessary thoughts.

How could he tell her? When? With what tone, with what words? In his house? On the walk back from the station? At the park halfway home? The more he thought about it, the more his mind wandered down alleys that led to nowhere. No answers.

If anyone else had ever faced a choice like this, he'd love to hear about it. This was a dilemma even fictional characters almost never had to deal with. The more he thought about it, the less real any of it was to him. He was beginning to think there was no right answer.

As his thoughts circled, the sun set and rose again. It was now Sunday. The day Mai finally had some space in her schedule.

But she'd already agreed to help with Kaede's makeover, so they were set to meet Mai at Fujisawa Station at two PM, after her morning's work was done.

That meant Kaede was with him.

At the meeting spot, they found a blond idol singer. Nodoka also had the day off. The four of them took the train two stations farther, to Chigasaki.

A hair and makeup artist who'd worked with Mai since the start of her career had started her own salon here.

It was a good ten-minute stroll from Chigasaki Station. You could really feel how close the water was.

The salon was very fancy. If Sakuta had been alone, he definitely would never have set foot inside. Small, but apparently doing good business.

"I could ask for no better endorsement than one from Mai Sakurajima," the owner said, grinning. She was a cool grown-up woman in her mid to late thirties, the kind of person who looked great in pantsuits.

They took Kaede right over to the mirrors. She looked nervous. The owner, Mai, and Nodoka all talked about different hairstyles with her. With each suggestion, the owner touched Kaede's hair, checking the volume and hair quality, giving her thoughtful advice.

There was never anything for Sakuta to do.

He sat on a couch and flipped a men's magazine open to an article on electronics he had no interest in. It was all about the latest smartphones and high-frequency music players. Every MSRP given was over fifty thousand yen. Most were closer to one hundred thousand. Not something a high school kid could reach for.

When he glanced in the mirror, he could see Kaede covered in sheets like a *teru teru bozu* while the owner's scissors snipped away. She still looked tense but was clearly hanging in there. She wasn't here because she had a crush on some guy. This was a major step on the path to getting her back in school.

He flipped through more magazines. Eventually, Nodoka came and sat next to him.

"I'll be coming right home after the concert on the twenty-fourth," she said.

"You should really hang out with your friends and enjoy the evening, Doka."

"Don't you call me that!"

"Then what should I call you?"

"Lady Nodoka."

"Treasure your fans, Lady Nodoka."

"G-God, don't actually do that!"

"No yelling in the shop, Lady Nodoka."

Several employees had looked at her, shocked.

"I—I said I'm coming right home!" she hissed, flinching away from him.

"We'll save some cake for you, Toyohama."

"That's not my concern."

She glared at him.

"Then…the Christmas chicken?"

"You're stuck on food, huh?"

"Like you're stuck on your sister?"

He didn't really expect that to work.

"Yep," she snapped. Apparently not the least bit interested in hiding it. Not that she ever had. After all, Nodoka Toyohama's official profile listed Mai Sakurajima as her favorite thing. It was out there for everyone to see. Sakuta still couldn't believe her agency had allowed it.

"Say, how's Mai been doing lately?" he asked, glancing Mai's way. She was standing behind Kaede, talking with her and the owner. She flashed a smile now and then, very elegant and mature.

The haircut was going smoothly.

"Not telling."

"Don't hold out on me, Doka."

"……"

"Lady Nodoka?"

"You really are blessed, Sakuta."

"Where'd that come from?"

"I mean, you get to spend Christmas with my sister!"

Her disgruntled look stabbed into his side.

"She's fussing about what to cook and where to get the cake and is trying hard to look her best, all for you!"

"That last one is also for work, though."

That was why she wore tights all summer, to avoid a tan.

"I never thought she'd spend so much time worrying over what to wear on a date."

"Now I'm jealous. I've never seen that side of Mai."

"Yeah, and she'll never let you."

"Just imagining it is adorable."

"Quit fantasizing about my sister!"

Nodoka tried to stomp on his foot, but he dodged.

"Don't move!"

"If you wanna step on me, take those boots off first."

They made a loud clicking sound every time she took a step and were surely classified as a lethal weapon.

"You let her step on you."

"Well, that's because she's Mai."

Only a weirdo would enjoy having their girlfriend's sister step on them.

"Stop trying!" he said, dodging again.

"This is a serious conversation!" Nodoka glared at him.

Sakuta was well aware of it, but he avoided her eye, pretending to read his magazine.

"I know," he said.

Sakuta knew exactly what lay ahead. Just a small glimpse of the future. And because he was painfully aware of it, no matter how much he wanted to…he couldn't promise not to make Mai cry. That wasn't a promise he'd be able to keep.

And he wasn't going to lie.

"……"

"Sakuta?"

Nodoka leaned in to look at his face. Her glittering gold hair filled his vision.

"Toyohama."

"What?"

"Your eyes are sparkling."

"They aren't. Dumbass."

"They totally are. Dumbass."

They bickered a few more minutes until the sound of the dryer subsided.

"All done!" the owner called.

The *teru teru bozu* costume was gone, and Kaede was getting to her feet. Slowly turning toward them.

She seemed to be struggling to make eye contact. Lots of fidgeting. Really childish behavior, but with her pigtails gone, her new hairstyle made her look much more grown-up. The length of her hair hadn't changed much, but it now curved gently inward, which gave it the impression of being shorter.

"I-is it weird?"

"Don't be rude."

"Th-that's not what I meant! I swear I didn't," she said, turning to the owner.

The owner was way too mature to care.

"I think it looks age appropriate," Sakuta said.

"Not like I'm trying too hard?"

"Kaede, that's Toyohama's department."

"Huh? How so?" Nodoka asked, blinking at him.

"This is what trying too hard looks like," Sakuta said as he squinted at her blond locks.

"It does not!"

"Your boyfriend's funny, Mai," the owner said.

Mai only managed an awkward smile. Didn't look like she'd taken that as a compliment.

"So? What *do* you think, Sakuta?" Kaede insisted.

"It's not too flashy, not too dorky, exactly where you want to be."

"G-good."

Still nervously rubbing her hands together, Kaede stole a couple more glances at herself in the mirror. There was a smile playing around her lips, so Sakuta was pretty sure she was quite taken with her new haircut. She just wasn't used to seeing herself with it and was too worried about everyone else's reactions to settle down. He figured she'd grow accustomed to it soon enough.

"You want a trim while you're here, Mai?"

"Oh, not yet. We're still filming."

"Just the tips won't show. And it is almost Christmas."

The owner shot a meaningful glance at Sakuta.

"I'll be on a bunch of shows doing promo work, so when that's over..."

She'd said she'd be out tomorrow and the next day, in Kanazawa again. Building hype for the movie by doing guest appearances on variety shows. One of which involved touring the filming location with the show's host. It was a major seven PM show, one Sakuta had watched before.

"You were just here last week, Nodoka," the owner said. "You should be fine for now."

"Yep."

"You go here, too, Toyohama?" Sakuta asked.

"That a problem?"

"You really do adore your sister."

"I love her way more than you do."

"Whoa, I can't let that pass unchallenged."

"I've got the advantage of years."

"Suuuure, fine. You win. Take care of her for me."

"Har?"

His attempt to be gracious was met with scorn. But Sakuta paid Nodoka no more attention. He'd felt eyes on him, and that was now dominating his thoughts.

"......"

Mai was watching Sakuta and Nodoka in silence. Even when his eyes met hers, she said nothing. He could feel the weight of her thoughts, but the whole time they were settling the tab and leaving the store, she didn't say a word.

The owner saw them out the door, and they headed back down the road to Chigasaki Station. Kaede spent the whole time bothered by how the wind was messing up her hair. And smiling happily every time Mai fixed it for her.

"Think you'll be able to touch it up yourself tomorrow?"

Sakuta pointed out that Mai couldn't exactly do it for her every day.

"If you do it the way she said, it'll be fine. Okay?"

"R-right..."

Kaede had been pretty nervous around the famous "Mai Sakurajima" at first, but the last few weeks had helped a lot. Now it was more like being around an older girl she really admired.

As they talked about this, they reached Chigasaki Station.

Mai headed toward the gates but stopped just outside.

"Nodoka, sorry—can you bring Kaede back home?"

"Mm? You can't?"

"I actually have plans with Sakuta."

This was news to him. He didn't remember agreeing to any such thing. She hadn't even sent him a nonverbal signal. He looked at her for an explanation, but she didn't meet his eye. She wasn't even looking in his direction.

But Sakuta had been planning to get her alone somehow anyway, so he fell in line.

"Kaede, think you can get home without me?"

"I can manage a lousy two-station train ride," she said, indignant. "How old do you think I am?"

"I think your body's third-year, but your mind's still first-year."

"I could have handled this whole day without you here, Sakuta. It was super embarrassing how you invited yourself along."

"I'm thrilled by your newfound independence."

"Don't glare at me!" Nodoka said.

"Siscon idol is sort of your whole thing."

"Like you're one to talk."

"Sorry, Kaede. I'm gonna borrow Sakuta for a bit."

"No problem. I dunno what you see in him, but he's all yours. Thanks for today." Kaede bowed her head. "Sakuta, uh…thank you, too, I guess," she added.

"You're welcome," he said, making it sound sarcastic.

"Ugh, you're such a jerk."

Kaede puffed out her cheeks.

"When'll you be back?" Nodoka asked, like it was an everyday event. Just setting expectations.

"Probably pretty late," Mai said evasively.

Nodoka shot Sakuta a reproachful glare. What did she think they were about to do here? Kaede was turning slightly red herself, so she *definitely* had the wrong idea.

But making excuses or trying to explain would just dig them in deeper, so he decided to let the misunderstanding stand. Revealing the truth would be way harder.

Mai didn't try to clarify things, either, so she must have reached a similar conclusion.

"......"

But her lips were tightly pursed, and he didn't recognize the emotions beneath that look. He thought about this as Kaede and Nodoka headed into the station, but ultimately he got nowhere. But he didn't need to. She'd secured them this moment alone so they could talk about it.

The question was where. He hadn't expected to end up alone with her at Chigasaki Station, so he had no clue where to go. He didn't ever come here and didn't know his way around. All he really knew about Chigasaki was that it was technically part of Shounan. So if they headed south, they'd reach the water. The salon had definitely seemed like it was close.

"It'll mean going back the way we came, but should we hit the beach?" he suggested.

But Mai was already gone.

"Huh?"

He found her over by the ticket booth. Looking up at the map of fares and lines.

"We going somewhere?" he asked, joining her.

"Yep."

"Where?"

"Far."

She walked off without him, heading toward the gates.

"Ah, wait up, Mai."

He ran after her.

She led him to the Tokaido Line platform. The same train they'd ridden here from Fujisawa Station. Going the other way would take them back home, but they were on the outbound side. This would take them to Odawara, Yugawara, and Atami.

"Where we headed, Mai?"

"The train's here."

He followed Mai onto an Atami-bound train without the slightest clue where she was taking him. It was a silver car with orange and green stripes on it.

They found some empty seats and sat down together. The doors closed, and the train pulled out of the station. It all seemed weirdly familiar. He and Mai had been on this train together before.

Last spring.

He'd met Mai and learned of her Adolescence Syndrome, and they'd ridden this train way out, trying to see how large the affected area was.

"Really takes me back," he murmured.

Mai didn't answer. Or meet his eye.

"Already been seven months."

"Still only been seven months."

"Life with you is so fulfilling, it makes time go faster," he said.

"......"

"I never thought I'd end up dating you then."

It wasn't like he hadn't been hoping. Spending time with a beautiful senpai was certainly enjoyable, and the fact that she'd give him the time of day at all never failed to make him giddy, but he hadn't really expected anything more. Or even thought about it. He'd just been savoring the time her Adolescence Syndrome had allowed them to spend together.

He'd spent a lot of time getting scolded for pushing his luck. She'd called him a snot. Sakuta himself was dogged by rumors about the hospitalization incident, but Mai had never paid those any attention. She'd only ever looked at him, judging him by what she saw, forming her own impressions.

So naturally, he'd felt comfortable around her. Even when she'd pinched his cheek or stomped his feet, it was Mai, so it was all fun. And he knew she wasn't doing any of that to hurt him. It was all part of their banter.

And that accumulated banter had become affection. And that affection had grown into love.

Mai and Sakuta had spent that much time together. The better part of a year. She'd made those months fun. Made them worth living. Allowed him to feel at ease.

Looking back on their shared history, Sakuta sat with Mai, putting those feelings into words. It was a fifty-minute ride to Atami Station, and for most of the journey, Sakuta was doing all the talking.

4

When they reached Atami Station, it was past six.

After sunset on a Sunday at a station known primarily for hot springs was not exactly crowded. Despite the hum of the heating units on the waiting trains, the station felt eerily quiet. The cold winter air might have added to that impression.

On the platform, Mai scanned both directions, looking for the timetable.

"......"

Her eyes scanned the numbers. She looked intense.

Didn't seem like Atami was her ultimate destination. They must've been headed somewhere even more distant. Maybe she was planning on taking them all the way to Ogaki, like they had last spring. But she hadn't joined him in his trip down memory lane at all.

"Which train will take us the farthest?" she asked. He was becoming more certain of his hunch.

"If we keep riding the Tokaido Line, we'll at least get to Ogaki."

They'd done exactly that before. Mai knew that. Going any farther would limit their options.

"If we switch to the Shinkansen, we could make it all the way to Osaka."

Only the Kodama stopped at Atami, but if they switched at Nagoya, they could board trains straight to San'yo or Kyushu. Trains that went so far west they turned south.

"What about this Izumo-bound train?" Mai asked, pointing at the timetable. It was a fairly late train.

"Izumo as in the *shrine* Izumo-taisha?" he asked.

"There's also one bound for Takamatsu."

"In Shikoku?"

That was Kagawa Prefecture. He checked the timetable himself, assuming there must be some mistake, but at 11:23 PM there were, in fact, trains bound for Izumo and Takamatsu. They both had sleeper cars listed, which explained the late-night availability. These were trains that headed out late and got passengers where they were going in the morning. If trains bound for two disparate locations started at the same time, then they likely traveled a chunk of the distance joined together.

All this meant that both Izumo and Takamatsu were indeed the super distant destinations he thought they were and not just something similarly named.

"If we take that train, we can go all the way to Izumo."

"I guess so."

He hadn't personally taken that train, but he had faith in the Japanese railway system.

"I wonder if you need a special ticket."

"Probably."

Mai took Sakuta's hand and started walking.

"Er...Mai?"

"......"

She just kept dragging him along.

"How far are we going?"

"To the station attendant."

"Not that... Our destination."

"Far."

"But how far?"

"Very far."

"......"

"If we keep riding trains, we can go even farther than last time."

"Sleeping cars are all the rage these days. We might not be able to get tickets."

This was a roundabout tactic, but it finally made her stop. She didn't turn back.

"Then we can take a normal train."

"That won't get us farther than Ogaki this late."

The schedule had been more or less unchanged.

"If we run out of trains, we can spend the night in some random town."

"Get a room together?"

"If you want."

"Sounds like a dream come true."

"And in the morning, we'll set out again."

"To somewhere far?"

"Yes, very far. As far as the two of us can get. So far we…"

She'd kept her voice flat this whole time, but suddenly he detected a quiver in it. She wasn't stifling her emotions, nor was she stoically unmoved. The emotions inside her were simply too powerful to express in a straightforward way. Sakuta knew this because he was feeling something very similar.

"Don't just give up."

"……"

"Don't just make a choice all on your own."

"I can't put this on you, Mai."

"What am I to you?"

When she said this, her eyes wavered. Like she hated herself for letting that out. Like it was something she never wanted to say aloud. But however much she'd sworn not to, her emotions had overridden her reason. She was past caring.

"My girlfriend."

"Then I'll bear that weight together with you…"

"……"

"Shouko's life..."

"......"

"As long as we're alive together..."

He gritted his teeth, glaring up at her.

"That hurts to hear, Mai."

"Why?!"

If Sakuta lived, that meant the heart transplant Shouko should have received would no longer happen. Maybe another donor would arrive, and Shouko's life would go on, but Sakuta didn't think the world was such a convenient place.

If his living meant Shouko would no longer be saved, how could he welcome that future with open arms? Little Shouko had worked so hard. Through all her suffering and pain, she'd struggled to stay positive and cheerful. It hurt to even think about changing her future just so he could live.

And he didn't want Mai to shoulder that pain. Neither of them was mature enough to live together burdened by that guilt. Even his limited moral compass wouldn't allow that.

And more than anything, Sakuta wanted to return the favor. Pay big Shouko back for what she'd done for him. She'd saved him two years ago, as well as a few weeks ago. She'd taught him what life meant. There was no way he could rob her of the most important thing there was.

"Sometimes even I have to do the right thing."

"You always do."

"If I don't, it's bad for everyone."

"Don't look at anyone but me, Sakuta!"

"I only made it this far because Kunimi and Futaba ignored the rumors and became my friends."

"......"

"Kaede made herself my sister, and I can't let her down. The original Kaede finally came back, and I can't do the wrong thing with her watching."

"Why… Why…?"

"Koga and Toyohama keep talking to me no matter how much I tease them. And Shouko saved me again and again."

"……"

"I don't want to be someone who disappoints the people who care about me."

"Even if I ask…?"

"I'll listen to anything you ask of me, Mai."

"Then…!"

"But right now, there's just one thing I can't do."

"Don't say that!"

Mai put her hands over her ears, like an angry child.

"Please," she whispered, staring at the ground. "Just be with me forever. Be at my side until Christmas is over."

"……"

"Never leave me."

She took a step forward and rested her forehead on his shoulder.

"Let's get on a train and go as far as we can go."

"That sounds like fun."

"Doesn't it?"

"If I could do that, I'd love to."

There was a note of resignation in his voice. He knew that wish would never be granted, which was what made it sound so tempting.

"But I can't, Mai."

"Why not?!"

"I've got school tomorrow."

Such an ordinary reason. Like something a mother would tell their kid.

"Skip."

"I've gotta get up and make breakfast for Kaede. You know Toyohama can't cook, either."

"……"

"And you've got work tomorrow, too."

"That doesn't..."

"You know what Toyohama said? No matter how high a fever Mai Sakurajima has, she never misses a day of work. No matter how crappy you feel, you'd wade right into the ocean in the middle of winter."

"...It doesn't matter. Work doesn't matter!"

"It does. People trust you. You can't let them down."

"If I lose you, then nothing else matters!"

Her hands clenched his jacket. Like she was never going to let go. That was why he kept talking. Being the voice of reason.

"I love you, Mai."

"......"

"And I love how you work."

"That's not important right now!"

"Every time I see you on TV or on a magazine cover, I think, 'My girlfriend's supercute.'"

"That's not what I wanted to hear."

"It's a shame you were always too busy to go on dates with me."

"I'm saying I'll never stop being with you again!"

"But I want to be with you the way you always are."

"......!"

This line really seemed to strike something deep within her. She gasped and went silent.

"Always strict with yourself, trying to be strict with me but actually being the opposite—that's the Mai I love."

As he said the words, he could feel a heat rising behind his eyes. A tingle behind his nose. He desperately fought it back, waiting for the wave of emotion to pass. If he cried here, it was all over. Everything he was struggling with would give way, and he'd start wanting to run away with Mai. To Izumo or Takamatsu, as far as they could get. But he couldn't do that. And so he had to beat the tears back.

"...Fine," she said when he fell silent.

"...Mai?"

"Fine."

"......"

"As long as you're alive, I don't care if you hate me!"

With untold emotions spilling out of her, she lifted her head.

When he saw that look on her face, Sakuta's mind went blank. Her eyes were overflowing with tears. Gushing down her cheeks, and all he could do was watch.

"Just...stay with me."

Mai was crying like a little kid, sniveling. There was no pretense of composure or beauty. She simply let everything out, holding nothing back. She slammed into him with the full force of what she was feeling.

"Just be with me..."

"......"

A wave of agonizing guilt tore through Sakuta. He had never imagined Mai crying like this. It had never occurred to him she even could.

He could feel his resolve wavering.

"Just be with me until Christmas is over. After that, you can hate me all you want!"

"I can't ever do that."

"Why not?!"

"I could never hate you."

"Why... Why...?"

Her legs gave way, and she crumpled. He knelt down, supporting her.

"I'll always love you, Mai."

He pulled her to him. Rubbing his hand on her back like he was soothing a crying baby.

"Liar..." Her voice was muffled by his shirt.

"I swear I'll always love you."

"Liar..."

"I'll love you forever."

"You're a liar…but so am I."

"……"

"I *do* care if you hate me."

Her grip on his shirt grew tighter. Pulling it so much it hurt.

"I don't want you to hate me," she sobbed.

And those were the last words she managed. Everything else was just tears. Unable to hold her tight, Sakuta let her sobs pound his ears like the lashes of the condemned.

5

They didn't talk on the train back to Fujisawa from Atami. They'd picked seats in the green car, trying to avoid prying eyes as much as possible, and Mai kept her eyes on the window.

They were red from all the crying, and since it was night, he could see that in her reflection. Sakuta fought off the urge to say something to her several times. If he let his guard down for even a second, the fragile shell would burst, and he'd tell her the thing he'd kept hidden.

And if he said that, there'd be no turning back. So he kept it secret, never giving voice to the thought.

It had taken a while for Mai to settle down at Atami Station, so by the time they got back to Fujisawa, it was after eleven. This late on a Sunday, the station was a lonely place. The Christmas lights everywhere only made it worse.

Neither Sakuta nor Mai said anything on the walk home, either.

Every now and then he heard her sniffling. They were walking side by side, not looking at each other but not splitting up, either. All the way to their apartments.

"Good night, Mai."

"Good night."

When they finally spoke, that was all they said.

Looking worn out, Mai went into her building. Sakuta waited until the doors closed behind her and she was out of sight. Then he turned and headed into his own building.

He was the only person on the elevator.

The silence was oppressive.

He could tell his grip on his emotions was starting to slip. The words he'd been trying so hard not to say were hovering around the back of his throat.

Keeping it out of mind had allowed him to remain functional. Not thinking about it had kept it out of sight. He'd never experienced death firsthand, which made him think he could handle it.

But seeing Mai cry had told him the truth.

He had seen what death meant in those tears.

The elevator reached his floor.

He dragged his feet down the hall to his door, turned the key, and stepped inside.

The lights were on. In the entrance, in the hall, and in the living room in back.

When she heard the door open, Shouko came out to see him.

"Welcome home, Sakuta."

The same old Shouko smile. Gentle and forgiving. It felt blinding. He turned his gaze downward.

"Mai's at home tonight?"

"Yeah…," he said, barely loud enough to hear.

"Ah."

"…Kaede?" he managed, not looking up.

"In bed. She really liked her new hairstyle! She's been grinning all night."

"Good."

"Bath first? If you're hungry, I can whip something up."

He tried to take his shoes off, but his legs wouldn't move.

"Shouko, I…"

When he finally lifted his head, she was still smiling.

"……"

Her face took his breath away.

"Don't," she said. "You've already got a lovely girlfriend."

Teasing him softly, keeping her voice down to avoid waking Kaede.

"Yeah, I could brag about her all night."

"Jealous."

"That's why…"

He couldn't hold out any longer. His voice cracked. A sob escaped his throat.

"I never wanted to make Mai cry like that."

It was such a simple idea, but putting it in words shook him to his core. It affected him far more deeply than he'd expected. A shock that started at his heart shot through his whole body.

He'd never thought he could feel anything this intense.

"I never want to make her cry like that ever again."

It was late. Kaede was in bed. He gritted his teeth, forcing his voice to stay quiet.

"That's why…Shouko."

Even as he broke down, Shouko just kept smiling.

"Yes? What is it?"

"I'm sorry, Shouko."

He couldn't meet her gaze. His whole body was shaking like a leaf. His knees buckled, and he dropped to the floor. He put his arms around himself, trying to stop the shaking, and let the feelings he'd kept deep inside escape.

"I want to live."

The shaking didn't stop. His body had never had to deal with anything like this before. So much fear, sadness, frustration…but Shouko was here. And her warmth.

"I want to go on living."

His heart's desire. Something so obvious it would never even enter his prayers. He'd never once had to ask for permission to live. There had never been a need. He'd taken life for granted.

But this same desire had been a constant in little Shouko's entire life. A single, basic wish. And one his imagination had never gotten anywhere near.

He wanted to live. That was all.

And that was why he'd felt it was wrong to wish for that in front of Shouko. Wrong to even say the words.

But such concerns couldn't stand up to the power of the desire rising within him. He had decided to put himself first. The more he tried to resist, the stronger the power fighting him. Until the need to live had forced its way out of him.

Because he loved Mai.

Because he didn't want her breaking down like that.

And if she had to cry, he at least wanted to be with her.

"I'm sorry, Shouko. I just… I'm sorry."

Nothing else came out of him. There was more he wanted to say. But like a child who doesn't know any other words, he simply kept repeating them.

"I'm sorry… I just want to be with Mai forever. Forever and ever."

Something warm wrapped around his shaking body. Shouko's warmth, embracing him, protecting him from everything that scared him.

"I'm the one who should be sorry," she said. "I'm sorry I forced this choice on you, Sakuta. If I'd played my cards right, you never would've had to suffer like this."

"That's not…"

"It's not your fault, Sakuta."

"I…"

"You did well, Sakuta."

"…But I!"

"You said everything you had to say."

"…Ah, aughhhhhh!"

He was past putting it into words.

"So make Mai happy."

"…Unhh…ahhh…aughhhhh!"

He wanted to say something to her. Gratitude? Apologies? Something else entirely? He wasn't sure, but he wanted to communicate *something.*

But nothing else came out of him. Not even tears. Just a long, raspy, wordless wail.

And Shouko forgave him for living.

Dye the white snow

1

Only two days remained before the future Shouko spoke of was upon him. Sakuta's mind spent that whole time making the same wish.

Wishing on the morning sun.

Wishing on the midday sky.

Wishing on the stars at night.

Wishing that little Shouko would be saved.

Sakuta wished upon the waters of Shichirigahama, the river flowing through his neighborhood, the shells on the beach, and the unidentified grass growing through the cracks in the pavement.

Please save little Shouko.

A fervent wish.

Sakuta couldn't cure her condition himself.

Wishing was all he could do.

Meanwhile, big Shouko showed no signs of worry, fear, or anxiety. She was perfectly calm. She accepted Sakuta's desire to live and stayed with him, smiling that impish grin the whole time.

If Sakuta wasn't hit by a car, little Shouko wouldn't get her heart transplant. That might mean the future that big Shouko came from would never happen. At the very least, the moment it wasn't Sakuta's heart being transplanted, her future would change.

That must have been a terrifying thought. But Shouko didn't show any signs of worry or fear. She was humming to herself as she cooked, cleaned, did the laundry, took a shower...

Twice they said, "Good morning," and twice they said, "Good night."

And like that, the two days passed by.

The sun rose, and it was already December 24.

The day of destiny. The stress of it may have helped Sakuta wake up on his own. He sat up and checked the clock. It was seven AM. The twenty-fourth. Christmas Eve.

Yawning, he hit the bathroom. Washed his face and gargled. He heard noises from the living room and poked his head around the corner in time to see Shouko in an apron, putting breakfast on the table.

"Good morning, Sakuta."

"Morning, Shouko."

"Come on, sit down."

She removed the apron and took a seat herself. There were two place mats on the table and food for two as well. Toast, ham, eggs, and sliced tomatoes.

Kaede was out, staying with their grandparents. Their father had stopped by yesterday afternoon to pick her up.

"Thanks."

"You're welcome."

"Did you sleep well?" Shouko asked, spreading jam on her toast.

"Sure… You?"

"Like a baby."

"You would."

"You can say that again!"

He'd intended it as sarcasm, but she was immune to that. She knew exactly what he meant but persistently spun his words in a positive light.

This was how every morning went since she'd moved in. Nothing changed until they were almost finished eating.

"Today's the last day we can be shacked up together. The end of all the smiles and blushes."

He started getting emotional again.

"Shouko..."

"You've already thanked me enough."

Sakuta shook his head. Naturally, he didn't think he could begin to thank her enough, but that wasn't what he wanted to say here. He had something else he needed her to hear.

"I wanted to be like you, Shouko."

"......"

"Two years ago, I was at rock bottom, and you came along and raised me up again. I wanted to be capable of random acts of kindness like that."

"You will be, Sakuta."

"No flustered denials?"

"If you admire me for it, then it would be rude not to own it."

This was a very Shouko way of thinking. Proof of her faith in those around her.

"Soy sauce."

"Huh?"

"Pass it this way?" She pointed with her fork. Not the best table manners.

Sakuta picked up the soy sauce and passed it to her.

"Thank you," she said.

"You're welcome."

She dribbled a few drops on the yolk, then took a big bite of ham and egg together. Her mouth full, she chewed for several moments, smiling blissfully.

"What?" she asked.

"Nothing."

"You're laughing."

"People do that when they're amused."

She must have liked that answer, because she laughed, too.

Maybe nobody else would have found this funny. But to the two of them, it was hilarious.

Unfortunately, they couldn't stay like that forever.

"You'd better go, Sakuta."

It was Christmas Eve, but he still had school. It was the last day of the second term, so it was just the end-of-term ceremony and a homeroom to get their report cards.

Sakuta changed into his uniform, and Shouko saw him off at the door, just has she had every other morning.

He turned back once his shoes were on.

"Shouko...," he started haltingly.

"Go on," she said.

Like she'd seen through that momentary hesitation. Like she was reproaching that moment of weakness. She put her hands on his back and gave him a push.

Her smile unchanged.

An impish grin.

As if even this little interaction was a source of such joy that it radiated from every inch of her body.

Sakuta only knew one way to respond to that.

So he said, "I'm off," like he was taking the first step into the future.

Just as he always did, so that Shouko wouldn't be worried about him. He even stifled a yawn as he opened the door.

And once he was outside, he didn't look back.

2

The people walking to the station all breathed puffs of white.

A little cloudy wisp appeared each time Sakuta exhaled as well.

The weather report last night had said there'd be record lows, below freezing even on the coast, and this morning was clearly living up to that. Even in sunlight, the temperature didn't noticeably improve. At best, it was in single digits. It was gonna be a real cold day.

And a cold front would move in that afternoon, making it snow as evening approached. The weather lady had been confident it would snow all evening. "Be prepared for traffic slowdowns," she'd added.

He looked up at the December sky, and it was a blue so pale it was almost clear. The light of the sun felt feeble. Shouko had said there would be a ton of snow that evening. There was no doubt in his mind she was right.

After a ten-minute walk, he reached Fujisawa Station and boarded a train for Kamakura. He stared out the window at the same old scenery until he reached Shichirigahama Station, where his school was.

The first minute or two after they pulled out of Fujisawa still felt like a commercial area, but by the time they reached the next station, they were well into the residential district. The farther they went, the calmer the streets, and as they drew near Enoshima Station, the sights took on a coastal feel. More and more walls painted white, aiming for that marine chic.

As the train continued on, the gap between the tracks and the buildings surrounding them narrowed. Near Koshigoe Station, the train was rolling slowly along, threading its way between houses built right up next to it. So close it seemed like the train might hit them. He was pretty sure branches from the trees in the yards did hit the cars sometimes.

And right as you started getting used to that, suddenly the whole view opened up.

The shores of Sagami Bay curved in either direction, the line of the horizon visible in the distance.

He saw this every day. It was no longer a surprise. The enthusiasm he'd felt the first time was long since gone. But it felt special today; if he had not known an accident lay in his future, this would have been his last time seeing it. The Sakuta from the older Shouko's future had seen this view without knowing any of that. He'd probably just yawned at it.

The thought made him yawn.

When they reached Shichirigahama, the tiny station platform grew packed with Minegahara students. Shuffling forward in unorganized lines, pouring out of the gates. Across a short bridge, over the railroad crossing, and into the school gates.

"Cold enough for you?"

"Too cold."

"It sucks!"

A group of girls were grumbling nearby. All of them had short skirts and bare legs, though. Cute is justice, anything else is the enemy—the daily battle of the high school girl raged on.

He didn't think they were being stupid. He just felt cold looking at them.

The whole student body gathered in the gym for the ceremony. Maybe the cold helped, because the principal kept his remarks blessedly short. Sakuta didn't remember a word he'd said, but he was probably just warning everyone studying for entrance exams to do their best not to get sick.

On the way back to their classrooms, Sakuta saw the third-years lined up in front of him. He searched for Mai but couldn't find her.

He knew he wouldn't. She wasn't at school today. If her schedule hadn't changed, she'd be at the studios in the city, filming the remaining scenes of her latest movie.

He hadn't seen her yesterday or the day before. They hadn't talked. He hadn't even heard her voice. He'd seen her on TV once or twice, but she'd been away from Fujisawa for work, sleeping in a hotel somewhere.

Sakuta had tried calling her a few times in the evening but only reached her voice mail. Mai never picked up or called back.

He figured she was intentionally avoiding him.

In class, homeroom started, and the teacher passed out their report cards. His teacher gave him a meaningful look, but he pretended not to notice. One glance at his results showed why. Every subject was a whole letter grade higher than the first term, which was guaranteed to get his teacher's attention.

"See you next year!"

And with that, homeroom was done, and like always, Sakuta left class without talking to anyone.

Most students were hanging around to chat, so the path to the station was still pretty deserted.

He got on the train and rode it back to Fujisawa Station.

Once he got there, he started to head home, but a few steps later, he paused and went in a different direction.

3

Sakuta's detour took him to the hospital where little Shouko was staying.

Room 301.

A quiet room. The only sounds coming from outside.

Shouko was in the ICU, but her things were still here.

Signs of life, but without the usual warmth he had grown accustomed to. Her presence felt further in the past each time he visited. Was that a trick of the mind?

"......"

He took a seat on the stool. When she'd still been here, he'd sat there every day, watching her earnest smile. He'd thought he could go on seeing that. Somewhere deep down, he'd been convinced she'd be okay.

The reason for that was obvious. He'd simply never had anyone close to him die. The grief he'd felt with Kaede's situation ought to have taught him what losing someone was like, but he just hadn't thought of Shouko that way.

He hadn't wanted to.

And perhaps the decisive factor was that Shouko had hidden her own fears until she was *really* in bad shape. She'd allowed him to avoid the truth.

At her age, going that far...maybe that was why Sakuta had been able to visit every day. Because she made it easier for him.

The older Shouko had talked like this was Sakuta's accomplishment, but he didn't think that was true at all. It all started with little Shouko's courage. Sakuta had just followed along.

"……"

He slowly got to his feet.

"I'll come again," he said, addressing the empty bed.

And then he left the room.

He took the elevator to the first floor.

As he passed the shop, his stomach growled.

Taking this as a sign, he stopped to buy a *yakisoba* roll and sat down on a couch in an unoccupied meeting room.

He peeled off the wrapper and took a bite. A fluffy roll packed with *yakisoba*. Double the starch, maybe a questionable aesthetic choice, but it tasted good at least.

This might well have been his last meal. That thought made him eat slower, trying to savor the flavor. But he was used to wolfing down meals like this, and it was hard to pace himself. He ended up inhaling it as usual.

As he popped the last bite into his mouth, a white coat passed by the door, then turned around and came back in.

"Thought that was you! Kaede's brother, right?"

It was the nurse who'd looked after Kaede.

"Were you looking for me?" he asked, confused.

The nurse's smile faded. "Shouko's mom said she wanted you to see her," she explained.

"……"

"She knows you've been visiting her empty room."

"Oh."

"Since her family's approved it, we can let you in. Are you up for it?"

"Does Makinohara want to see me?"

He thought little Shouko would probably rather not let him see her in the ICU.

"She's asleep, so you don't need to worry there."

That meant he was probably right.

"Well?" she asked again.

But Sakuta had already made up his mind. He had the moment she suggested it.

"I'll see her."

He felt like he should know. Felt like it was his responsibility to bear witness to what she was going through.

"Then come this way."

She led Sakuta down to the end of a long hospital corridor. Through two clinical white automatic doors was a plain room. It said PREP ROOM on the doors, and he was asked to leave everything but valuables in a locker here. He took off both his coat and his uniform blazer and was given some sort of apron. Wearing a mask and a lunch-lady hat was also mandatory.

Then he washed his hands thoroughly. They applied disinfectant afterward, with the nurse checking him over carefully, and he was finally allowed to set foot in the ICU.

Even then, the rule was that only her family were actually allowed in the room. The most he could do was look through the glass.

"Shouko's in here."

At first, Sakuta wasn't sure where she was. All he could see through the glass was a stack of medical machines.

It took several seconds of searching before he found Shouko. Her bed was surrounded by medical apparatuses, but that was definitely little Shouko lying there.

"……"

He gulped.

A jolt of pain shot through his chest.

He could hear some sort of pump working. A beep marking her pulse. A hiss of air escaping. It struck him that all these machines were sustaining Shouko's life.

It made him want to look away. If not seeing this was an option, he'd gladly take it. But Sakuta didn't look away, didn't let himself.

Shouko was doing her best to stay alive at that very moment, and he had to burn that into his retina.

"She's really something," he said at last. "Makinohara's still hanging in there."

She'd been fighting this whole time. All along. Against her condition, against an unfair world, against fate itself. She was still fighting now. For her future, for her parents' smiles, for everyone who'd supported her.

"She's really..."

And that was why, when it was all over, he had to tell her.

You did good.

He wanted to lavish praise upon her.

The words she deserved to hear.

He was shaking. His heart was quivering. And he was fighting that, gritting his teeth, clenching his fists, biting back the tears.

He wasn't sure what those tears were for. But he was on the verge of losing control.

Sakuta did everything he could to maintain his composure. He couldn't start crying in front of Shouko.

The five minutes he was allowed to see her was over in no time.

"I know it's not long, but it is the rules."

"Of course."

The nurse escorted him back out of the ICU.

He turned back once at the last second, but Shouko's eyes never opened.

In the prep room, he took off the apron, threw the hat and mask away, and collected his things from the locker. He thanked the nurse and was sent back into the main hospital.

Sakuta didn't really remember what he did for a while after that.

He felt like he'd been thinking about something but had no memories of what.

When the lights in the hospital hall turned on, he snapped out of it.

He was sitting on a bench by the vending machines.

He looked up at the window; it was dark out.

His eyes turned, searching for the time, and found a large clock on a pillar.

It was past five. He looked again, and it wasn't *that* dark outside. It just looked darker because of the clouds, but there was still *some* light in the sky.

Still, while he'd been lost in thought, over three hours had passed.

He couldn't hesitate any longer. Sakuta quietly stood up.

His feet took him to the public phones next to the vending machines. He found some coins in his wallet and picked up the receiver. He dropped a few coins in and reached for the number pad.

Normally, he punched these eleven digits in happily, but today his finger was trembling, and he had to take it one button at a time.

When he finally finished, he put the receiver to his ear.

Counting the rings. One ring, two, three…

On the fifth ring, the call picked up. Based on his attempts the last two days, Sakuta was sure it had gone to her answering machine.

A moment later, the usual message played. Standard "At the sound of the tone, leave a message."

"It's me. Sakuta."

The hospital corridor was so quiet, his voice echoed slightly.

"……"

He couldn't think of anything else to say. He must have had something in mind when he decided to call, but nothing was coming out.

Maybe he'd never had anything to say. Perhaps he'd just wanted to hear her voice. Sakuta felt that was something he would do.

"I really do love you, Mai," he whispered, laughing at himself for it.

But as he said it, there was a click on the line. Someone picking up. He soon knew who.

"Sakuta?" Mai's voice said.

"Mai."

"……"

"……"

"Yesterday…"

"Mm?"

"I had a dream."

"…You did?"

Sakuta didn't know where this was going. Mai was talking like she was addressing someone very far away, and he couldn't get a read on her emotions.

"Yes. A dream."

"What kind?"

"The two of us were visiting a shrine for New Year's."

"......"

"In the dream, we went on the last day of winter vacation, trying to avoid the crowds."

"What a scrupulous dream."

"I know."

"What did you wish for?"

"You bragged out loud that you'd wished for my happiness."

"Sounds like me."

"Yeah, even in my dreams, you're still a liar."

She laughed softly.

"But...Sakuta."

"Mm?"

"I love you anyway."

"......"

He couldn't speak. He just stood there, phone pressed to his ear. So focused he could hear every breath she took.

"So I'm not going to forget you, Sakuta."

"......"

"I'm going to live with you."

"Mai, I..."

He wasn't sure what he was trying to say. And before he could say it, the call cut off. Not because Mai had lost her signal, but because Sakuta hadn't put enough coins in.

"......"

He didn't have any more coins. He could probably break a larger bill if he bought a drink, but...he didn't.

He didn't have time to talk to her anymore. The longer he listened to her voice, the more the scales would tip toward her. And that would feel like he was making it her fault.

It had to be his choice.

He had two wishes, and he wanted both of them to come true more than anything.

He wanted Shouko to be saved.

And he didn't want Mai to cry.

If standing here thinking wouldn't get him an answer, he had to start walking.

He could head toward the spot he and Mai had agreed to meet for a date.

The aquarium near Enoshima.

He felt sure that as the moment neared, everything else would fall away, and only his true desire would remain.

He had faith in that. This choice was too important.

So he faced forward and started walking.

4

Near Fujisawa Station, the department stores and station buildings were all covered in Christmas lights. Very much in the holiday spirit.

It was already snowing when he left the hospital, and it was coming down even harder now. Really bringing that silent night, holy night vibe. There were lots of couples standing still, gazing up at the lights, and this made the area around the station feel much more crowded.

Squinting his eyes at these sights, Sakuta found himself oddly at peace.

He passed through the crowd of couples and headed for the Odakyu Line. He ran his train pass through the gate, brushed the snow off his shoulders, and stepped onto a local train bound for Katase-Enoshima.

Given the time they'd agreed to meet, Sakuta probably would have been on this train, riding it in blissful ignorance.

After a few minutes, the departure time arrived. The bell rang, the doors closed, and the train slowly pulled out of the station.

There were empty seats, but he stayed standing.

From his spot by the doors, he glanced around the car interior. Lots of couples. It *was* a major date holiday. They were likely headed to the same place Sakuta was. To Enoshima to look at the Sea Candle or the jellyfish light show at the aquarium—maybe both.

The train stopped at two stations on the way, Hon-Kugenuma and Kugenuma Beach. The snow didn't slow the train down at all; it carried Sakuta to Katase-Enoshima Station in less than ten minutes.

The doors opened slowly but noisily, and Sakuta stepped out onto the platform, snowflakes swirling all around.

He joined the throngs filing out of the gates. As he scanned his train pass, the display showed only sixty-two yen remaining. Not enough to get back home.

Sakuta turned toward the ticket booths and inserted his pass card. Then he took a one-thousand-yen note out of his wallet and charged that amount to the pass.

Maybe he didn't need to worry about getting home, but if he hadn't known what the future held, Sakuta would definitely have added funds here. Since he still wasn't sure which way his emotions would lead him, he had to be ready for anything.

With the funds loaded onto the card, it popped back out of the machine. He put it back in his wallet and headed south. Toward the water. He'd agreed to meet Mai outside the aquarium, which was on the coast.

There was a faint dusting of snow on the sidewalk. Free of any unnecessary thoughts but watching his step, he headed toward the aquarium.

One step after another, moving at the same speed he always did. He soon reached Route 134, which ran along the coast. To his right, he could see the aquarium. All he had to do now was cross the street.

The light had been green, but it started flashing. When he saw that, a pain shot through Sakuta's heart. A jolt that pulsed through his entire body.

Sakuta's brain was urging him to beat the light.

Route 134 was a major expressway. Once the light turned red, it would be a long wait. Years of experience had taught him it was best to cross while you had a chance, even if you had to run for it.

"......"

But despite his best efforts, his feet wouldn't budge. It was like they were sewn to the pavement. A couple raced past him, and all he could do was watch them go.

The light stopped flashing and turned red. The last couple made it safely across. They were out of breath from that short run and laughing about it. He watched them head toward the aquarium, clearly enjoying themselves.

The line of cars waiting for the light started pulling out, and he lost sight of the happy couple. Sakuta watched the taillights of the cars headed toward Shichirigahama. Scanning for any signs of a car skidding on the snow. None seemed to be having any trouble.

His back felt clammy. He'd assumed this was where he was most likely to get run over. The sidewalks here were smoothly paved and quite wide, so he'd imagined if he made it to the coastal side, there'd be little risk of a car sliding into him.

He kept watching the cars racing past, but no matter how long he observed, none of them were slipping.

Maybe it would happen when the light changed again.

"......Whew."

He hadn't realized how relieved he was until the sound escaped him. But he wasn't sure what he was relieved about. Because he was still alive? Because the accident still hadn't taken place? Maybe both...or maybe neither.

Still uncertain, Sakuta turned his eyes to the walk light. If he failed to cross this time, he'd be late—he'd never make it to the aquarium by six. That was how long the lights here kept you waiting.

He glanced toward the aquarium. Normally, he'd already be there. It was so close he could reach it in less than ten seconds if he ran for it. But if he headed there, Sakuta would never reach his destination. A car would skid in the snow and hit him.

He let out another long sigh. He still hadn't made a clear choice, and trying to stifle his fear, he took a deep breath.

Then he looked at the light again.

It turned green.

He saw it change through the cloud of his breath.

The crowd waiting under the frigid skies started moving. Passing on either side of Sakuta as he stood rooted to the spot.

The crowd moving in the other direction reached him, and the two flows merged, mingling.

Sakuta still didn't budge.

It wasn't fear making him hesitate. It wasn't because his body had chosen to live. He'd seen a light to his left, out of the corner of his eye, that was far brighter than the traffic signal.

Enoshima. Floating out there on the water.

The Sea Candle rose like a lighthouse, all lit up for Christmas. The sight of it had distracted him so much he forgot to cross.

There must have been a ton of couples gathered at the base of it, whispering "It's so pretty," spending a special day together.

Sakuta remembered that he might have been among them.

——*"Take me to see the Enoshima Illumination on Christmas Eve."*

The older Shouko's request.

"......"

And that recollection had made him consciously stay put.

There was a doubt in his mind.

He wasn't sure how long it had been there, but now that he was aware of it, it was growing rapidly.

Back then, the day they toured the wedding venue. If Shouko hadn't asked him to join her for a Christmas Eve date—what would have happened?

Where would Sakuta and Mai have planned their date?

——*"How about the illumination show on Enoshima?"*

That had been Mai's initial suggestion.

But because it was the same place Shouko had proposed, Sakuta had suggested the aquarium instead. Insisting he would like jellyfish if he was seeing them with Mai.

"......"

The pieces fell into place in hindsight.

And this fact was making his heart race.

He'd been wondering for a while.

Why was it Shouko could smile like that?

Even when she'd told him the truth.

Even when he'd told her he wanted to live.

Even this morning, he'd wondered how she could be so at peace.

It all made sense now.

Shouko had already done what she had to do.

To save Sakuta.

For that simple purpose, Shouko had done everything she set out to do.

——*"I'll be waiting at the dragon lantern by the entrance to Benten Bridge at six* PM *on December twenty-fourth."*

That was it.

She'd said she'd wanted one last memory, but that was an excuse to hide her real motivation. Maybe it was also how she really felt, but she'd used that for her ultimate goal.

To keep Sakuta away from the scene of the accident.

That was why Shouko had asked him on a date. And even specified where they should meet. Specified the time.

If she did that, she knew Sakuta would stay well away from there. She had faith that he'd choose Mai. Trusted that he'd turn her down.

Even if Sakuta chose a future where he'd die, it wouldn't actually matter. Even if he went to his date with Mai at the aquarium, nothing would happen. Because the accident took place somewhere else.

"But that means..."

A shiver ran up his legs. Like a wave washing over him. It reached his head and left his eardrums humming.

It was all for this moment.

When she'd said…

——*"It'll all be over by Christmas."*

Or…

——*"If I'd played my cards right, you'd never have had to suffer like this."*

Or even when she'd smiled and said…

——*"Go on."*

He knew now what she'd been hiding.

"How…?" he gasped.

It boggled the mind.

How could she go that far for someone? For Sakuta?

"What are you *doing*, Shouko?"

His feet left the ground. His body moving before he knew it.

His feet slipped on the snow, but he didn't care. He ran as fast as he could.

Maybe it was too late.

Maybe he could still make it if he ran.

He didn't know, so he ran as fast as he could.

His breath was white.

The freezing air made his nose and lungs burn.

But he kept running. He could see Enoshima. Still quite a distance away.

Shouko was probably waiting for him in front of Benten Bridge.

It was almost six, the time they'd agreed to meet.

He had maybe a minute or two left.

——*"Sakuta promises to meet you for a date, and on his way there…a car skids on some ice."*

If what Shouko had said was true, his fate would be decided in the next couple of minutes.

"Haaah…haaah…"

He threw himself through the snow swirling across Katase Bridge. He could see Benten Bridge on the other side. But the Sakai River was rather wide, and it still felt like a long way.

He was panting hard. Almost ran straight into someone. "Sorry!" he yelled but kept on running. No time for anything else.

He couldn't let it end like this.

This wasn't how it should end.

He was done being the only one saved.

So he threw every last ounce of strength into this mad dash.

Across the Sakai River.

Benten Bridge was on the other side of the road.

During the day, he would already have been able to see the dragon lantern she'd mentioned.

But Route 134 was in the way. There wasn't a signal here. He couldn't cross.

There was a pedestrian underpass burrowing beneath the road.

He realized he'd just run right past it.

He tried to stop and turn back.

And a horn sounded behind him. Coming his way.

"!"

He turned in time to see a car skidding sideways.

A black minivan.

Skidding in the snow.

Barreling right toward him.

"Sakuta!"

Someone screamed.

His head snapped toward the voice, and he saw Shouko across the street. Her eyes asking, "Why?"

When their gazes met, Sakuta smiled, almost in resignation.

Something black blocked his view. The sliding minivan came between them.

This was it.

But even as the thought crossed his mind…

"Sakuta!"

He recognized that voice.

Something soft hit him, shoving him to one side.

Then he heard a dull thud behind him.

Sakuta found himself lying facedown on the asphalt. His hands cold from the snow. Bleeding from the scrapes on his palms. The pain and cold forced his mind into motion again. He was still alive. Alive, but sore and chilled to the bone.

What had happened?

How was he not dead?

His mind reeled.

He picked himself up.

He heard gasps going up from the people around him. People crowding close.

Around Sakuta, the minivan…and someone else.

The black minivan had hit a street sign, knocking it over. His ears finally registered the sound of the blaring horn.

Someone was on the ground next to him. Bathed in the glow from above, like a spotlight shining down on her stage.

"……"

Sakuta's mouth moved. But no sounds came out.

There, on the faint dusting of snow…

…that cold, wet carpet, dyed red with blood.

With Mai's blood.

"I want you to choose a future with me."